Charles Gulland

Rothesay

A drama in three acts

Charles Gulland

Rothesay
A drama in three acts

ISBN/EAN: 9783337303617

Printed in Europe, USA, Canada, Australia, Japan

Cover: Foto ©Andreas Hilbeck / pixelio.de

More available books at **www.hansebooks.com**

ROTHESAY:

𝔄 𝔇𝔯𝔞𝔪𝔞

IN THREE ACTS.

By G.,

AUTHOR OF "THE LOMOND HILLS," ETC. ETC.

EDINBURGH:

GEORGE DRYDEN, 54A LOTHIAN STREET.

1883.

DRAMATIS PERSONÆ.

KING ROBERT OF SCOTLAND.

ANNABELLA, his Queen.

DUKE OF ROTHESAY, their Son.

SIR JOHN RAMORNIE.

SIR WILLIAM LINDSAY of Rossie.

DUKE OF ALBANY, Rothesay's Uncle.

EARL OF DOUGLAS.

ARCHIBALD DOUGLAS.

ELIZABETH DOUGLAS, afterwards Duchess of Rothesay.

EARL OF MARCH.

ELIZABETH, Lord March's Daughter.

CATHERINE GRAEME.

HOST OF THE CASTLE INN, Falkland.

JOHN WRIGHT, JOHN SELKIRK, WARDENS, GIPSIES, ATTENDANTS, &c. &c.

Scene—Various parts of Scotland.

ROTHESAY.

ACT I.

SCENE I.—*In the Street, before Falkland Castle.*

Enter DUKE OF ROTHESAY.

ROTHESAY.—What !   Warder, ho ! open the castle gate,
I would an audience of Duke Albany.
No answer, and no stir? this frowning pile
Courts slumber early.   [*Knocks loudly.*
                    Warder, warder, ho !
Art gone to sleep?   Ah ! would that I could sleep
The slumber of the just, ere kindly night
Casts her broad mantle o'er the vexéd world.
For me, this is the quickest, busiest hour
Of all day's busy round.   Open, I say,
Else will I rouse the townsfolks to confound
Thy coveted repose.
                    [*Knocks again, and the Warder appears
                         inside the gate.*
WARDER.—Begone !   You cannot enter here to-night.
ROTHESAY.—Thou'rt saucy, knave.   I seek Duke Albany.
WARDER.—The duke has gone to rest.   The garrison
Are all abed.   The curfew-bell has tolled.
The folks are housed, all saving silly lads
And love-lorn maids, and suchlike cumberers
Whose deeds excuse the honest face of day.
Come on the morrow, sir; but now, Good e'en.   [*Is retiring.*
ROTHESAY.—Stay, I command.   Warder, you know me not.
The Duke of Rothesay would have entrance here,
To commune with his grace of Albany.
WARDER.—Were you the King himself, I would refuse.
My lord and master is Duke Albany ;
And this his bidding, " When the curfew tolls,
The castle gates are closed."

ROTHESAY.—   But not to me !
    Go ! tell your master that I stand outside
    And would admission.
WARDER.—   I must say thee, Nay ;
    Good e'en, lord duke.   [*Retires.*
ROTHESAY.—Go, churl ; may Satan rob thee of thy rest !
    My precious uncle, my sweet Albany,
    This is your work ; insult to insult added.
    What next, I wonder ?   Do I hate this man,
    This brother of my father ?   Surely, no.
    It were unworthy me to foster hate,
    And yet I love him not.   What, am I wroth
    Because he turns me back on slight pretence ?
    Nay, let me treat the matter lightly ; let me
    To hospitable action shame him.
                        Yonder stands
    The Tolbooth, well I know it ; from its wall
    An iron chain depends, that bids the bell
    Summon the townsfolks to their early toil,
    And to their labour's close.   I'll to the bell,
    And with unwonted clamour startle forth
    The honest villagers.   [*Rings briskly.*
                  Never, O never,
    Rang I so sweetly in the stilly hour
    As now ; and yet I do remember me
    This is my first essay, and I do boast
    When thus I praise myself.   I'll change the tune
    Upon my listeners, and toll a knell
    Will make the timid tremble in their beds,
    And bid them, anxious, to their orisons.   [*Rings slowly.*
    And now, a wedding-peal.   [*Rings briskly.*
                Ha ! steps approach,
    The Falconland awakes, and would inquire
    Whence this unwonted clamour.

Enter from the Castle the DUKE OF ALBANY *and certain of the garrison,*
    and from their homes several of the townsfolks.

               My lord duke,   [*To Albany.*
    You honour me in coming forth to-night
    To welcome me.   For you, my honest folks,   [*To the towns-*
    If with sweet music I have pleased your ears,   *folks.*
    I make you free and welcome to my art ;
    And for your recompense in braving thus
    The chills of night, withdraw ye to the inn.
    Mine host will in my name—Duke Rothesay speaks—
    See to your comfort.   I'll be there anon.   [*The townsfolk*
    And now, my lord, you would a word with me ?   *withdraw.*
    Say on.
ALBANY.—What madcap prank is this ?   O nephew mine,

When will you cease this folly? when remember
  Your high estate?
ROTHESAY.—'Twas folly, sure, to pass your castle gate
  And meet your meanness with a sportive act.
  Sir, I am Lord-Lieutenant of the kingdom,
  Next to my royal sire, who delegates
  To me his high authority.   When I
  Come to this castle, held for us by you,
  And seek admission, but demand in vain,
  Then are you most disloyal and untrue
  To your high trust, your monarch, and to me.
ALBANY.—Shall proper watch and ward be not observed
  Because my nephew wanders late o' nights?
  Whence come you, royal sir?
ROTHESAY.—   A weary way;
  But welcome such as yours foils weariness.
ALBANY.—Welcome, your grace, to Falkland, to your own;
  Although the Lomonds and our spacious park
  May scarce afford the sport that Rossie gives
  A royal visitor.
ROTHESAY.—   I understand
  Your taunt.   That you do hate me, Albany,
  I know; but you are impotent and mean;
  And what of venom harbours in your sting
  Is purposeless for harm.   Leave my amours
  To be discussed by younger men than you;
  And leave the tales that silly gossips tell
  For idle women, sir.   And now, adieu,
  I go to seek my lodging in an inn.
ALBANY.—Stay, stay, your grace, this may not, cannot be.
ROTHESAY.—I shall not lodge in Falkland Tower this night.
  When next I deign to enter yonder walls
  'Twill be as Lord-Lieutenant of the realm,
  My guard behind me, and my pennon raised,
  The emblem of my state; and woe to him
  Who dares oppose my way.
ALBANY.—I do entreat you, be my guest to-night;
  .And pardon me if I have done amiss.
ROTHESAY.—I pardon you, but am resolved to lodge
  Without the castle walls; and so, adieu!   [*Exit.*
ALBANY.—Go, haughty lad, the time may come, and soon
  When you will be the guest of Albany;
  Then shall your state and food and lodging be
  Apportioned to your merit and high rank!
  Poor youth! you know not whom you trifle with.
  Expert and quick of fence he needs to be
  Who would oppose him to Duke Albany.
  But more of this anon; retire we now,
  The evening wears, and this ill-mannered freak
  Of Scotland's royalty mars discipline.   [*Exeunt.*

SCENE II.—*Falkland, before The Castle Inn.*

Enter SIR JOHN RAMORNIE *and* CATHERINE GRAEME.

SIR JOHN.—But I love you, Kate; I tell you I love you, and so ardently, that when you are not beside me I pine for melancholy. There is a weight upon my heart, Kate, that bids fair to prostrate me utterly unless you smile upon my suit. My horse, my hawk, my hound, my former pleasures, are uncared for now! The very face of Nature ceases to smile for me, because I possess you not. Ah! Love, Love, thou art a wanton, whom I would not kill, not even for all the pain thou hast caused me!

CATHERINE.—'Tis the old tale, Sir John. Men are like children, they pine for a new toy; but when possessed, it is soon wearied of, and cast away.

SIR JOHN.—Nay! Were I to acquire a pearl of price, I should ever keep it, and wear it proudly and carefully. Sweet Kate, leave this retired home of yours, and come abroad into the busy world with me. You shall be my pearl of price, and men shall envy me the brilliant I possess.

CATHERINE.—You would marry me, then, Sir John?

SIR JOHN.—Marriage is a ceremonial whose nature I have not yet learned to interpret. What is marriage? a few words uttered, a few responses said, signs made and symbols given, and lo! the twain are man and wife. But can marriage be composed of such materials? Nay! Love, mutual love, *is* marriage; and such love I promise you, as shall rivet the marriage chain more firmly than all the priests in Christendom.

CATHERINE.—I understand you, sir; but by your own telling, without mutual love there can be no marriage. You love me, but I love you not; and so I say nay to your offer, and bid you—adieu!

[*Exit.*

SIR JOHN.—Perseverance, they say, levels mountains. I'll be even with the jade ere long, unless, indeed, the Prince has been beforehand with me there. But here he comes.

Enter ROTHESAY.

Good-day, Lord Duke, good-day.

ROTHESAY.—Methinks I observed a tight-fitting bodice, and a gay kirtle, with a neatly-turned pair of ankles, vanish like a shadow as I approached. Ah, friend of mine, and mentor mine, is this your philosophy?

SIR JOHN.—The shrewdest philosophy I am acquainted with. *Carpe diem*, the ancients preach, and I admire the literature of the past.

ROTHESAY.—True, and I myself am an apt pupil in construing the classics; indeed, although Ramornie be the older man, I vow that Rothesay is the more successsful lover. You are over-serious, friend, when you converse with the sex; over-serious, and over-sedulous to please. Woman is never more easily captivated than when she deems that she herself requires to captivate. This is the great secret, and for now imparting it you ought to return to me a word of thanks. But whence come you?

RAMORNIE.—I am resident with Duke Albany at the Castle here, and learning that you are lodging in the town, I sallied forth to meet my Prince and patron. We heard of your junkettings with the towns-folks last night, after your refusal to enter the Castle; and I promise you the Duke is in a white glow of wrath at what he terms your undignified doings.

ROTHESAY.—Let the Duke attend to his dukedom, while I govern my principality. He knows not his position, and shall be made to realise it before the moon has waned. What! he, forsooth, would censure me! he, the ancient dotard, whose blood runs cold in his veins, and whose temper is soured because my royal father hath issue of his body! Listen to me, my friend. Since I have been entrusted with the lieutenancy of the kingdom, say, how goes it? Fairly on the whole, I vow. The people grumble not; thievery is becoming rare, so are contentions and broils. The nobles hunt, while the commons toil; and we are at peace with the nations. As for myself, when I show me abroad, I am met with the open countenance, the smile, and the clamour of welcome. Depend upon it, if one governs young, one must govern cheerfully, and take the people as it were into confidence. But were my uncle to govern, forsooth, then would the reign of gloom and terror begin. The noble would fret in his stronghold, or war with his peer; the labourer would hesitate to cast his grain into the soil; and our adversaries abroad would send forth a screech of defiance against haughty Scotland. But all this by the way. I weary you with my dissertation, yet would have you to know, that although I be careless, there is more thought under my bonnet than my sage uncle ever dreams of when he condescends to sneer at the madcap Rothesay.

RAMORNIE.—I know your abilities, my lord, for you admit me to the proud position of friend and confidant; yet would I have you sober down and wed, because although young in years, you hold a grave position, and were born to lofty responsibilities.

ROTHESAY.—Responsibilities! a lofty-sounding word. Yet though men in high places are declared responsible, I never see them pay up when loss ensues; there is ever a scapegoat. Remember, 'tis the way of the world, and I shall pass through it as well as another. And *you* would recommend me to wed? *you*, whom I have but now detected in close commune with some light-footed lass? Ah, Sir John, Sir John! I vow you are uneasy at my repeated successes with the fair. My poor friend, pray admit that I have sorely overshadowed you, and fully defeated you in the lists of love since first we became boon companions and friends. You recollect—? but, no, I shall not continue.

RAMORNIE.—Continue, and welcome; but, I remind your highness, that 'tis my bounden duty in such matters to give place to the blood-royal of Scotland.

ROTHESAY.—Tush! tush! there spake jealousy. Well do you know that I am no conceited shallow fool; but I must needs remind you that, not in love affairs alone, but in such as concern a well-graced knight, I am well trained, and of as good parts as any in the realm. Which of our young nobility can I not ride against? tilt, joust, and wield the sword against? Can I not dance, leap, and sing better than yourself? and who, pray, was my teacher and director-general in such affairs? Yourself, Ramornie, yourself. Only the pupil now surpasses his master, and that master must now content him to remain in the background. However, let this pass. I speak overmuch about my own merits, and the practice of boasting is wrong in principle; but I am strangely elated to-day. But see! a motley company approaches.

Enter a Band of Gipsies and Morris Dancers, who salute.

Now strike up music, and to the dance, my friends. I am no mean judge, observe you, and shall censure faults.   [*Music—they dance.* Excellently well danced, my friends. And who be you, my tall fellow, for I see you take the lead here?

GIPSY.—I am the King, may it please you, Sir.

ROTHESAY.—The King! Ha! I fear your monarchy is limited. Methought there was but one king in fair Scotland, the good King Robert.

GIPSY.—But truly, sir, he is a bide-at-home kind of king, his realm is within doors; mine is in the wood, on the moor, and on the mountain side. Yonder Lomond Hill is my throne, when I choose to sit in state; but I fear good King Robert never could hirple to its summit, and therein am I a better king than he.

ROTHESAY.—Enough on that score, friend, an' you would have me keep the peace. Now tell us, O King, is Her Majesty the Queen present among your people?

GIPSY.—Ay, truly; shall I bid her advance?

ROTHESAY.—Nay, nay! My friend here and I are ardent admirers of beauty, and if you can tell me she carries the palm among the women of your tribe, it will pleasure us to detect Her Majesty without your help. Is she beautiful?

GIPSY.—Beyond them all, if a husband may say so much about his wife without turning her head. But there they stand; now let your tongues proclaim the judgment of your eyes.

SIR JOHN (*leading forward a Gipsy girl by the hand*). — This, and none other, is the Queen, I vow. (*The Dancers laugh derisively.*) Tell me your name, sweet lass?

GIRL.—My name is Marion, sir, but I am no queen, nor do I aspire to royalty.

SIR JOHN.—If beauty, Marion, were royalty, then art thou royal here.

ROTHESAY (*leading forward another Gipsy girl*). — Where be your eyes, Sir John? Behold the Queen! (*She smiles and signifies assent.*) Ha! could I be deceived? You walk a queen, your every gesture betrays you; and in token of my admiration, I venture to to kiss the cheek of Nature's Majesty. And now, Sir John, I have detected a queen, and for my shrewdness have received my reward.

Did not I say, and with cause, that the pupil hath beaten his master?

SIR JOHN.—But the master shall receive his reward also. Kiss me, Maid Marion, for my courtesy and for my misjudgment.

MARION.—Nay, nay! Kissing comes not from my side of the house.

SIR JOHN.—Then I shall steal a kiss from the fairest woman among this company.

GIPSY.—Nay, I love not to see a man steal; for, to speak plainly, we Gipsies like to keep the art of stealing (a true art) among ourselves. *Snatch* a kiss, if you will, and if the lass allows it.

MARION.—No, no! He is a black ill-conditioned man, and if kissing is to be the fashion, I'd rather have a buss from his neighbour.

ROTHESAY.—Bravely spoken, lass, and to be bravely acted on.

[*Advances.*

SIR JOHN (*interposing*).—This shall not be! Stand back, my lord, you are ever high-handed, and presume upon your place to affront your comrades; stand back, I say, I brook no interference here.

ROTHESAY.—Well, well, keep down your choler; 'tis a mistake even to show anger. Let the better man kiss the lass, and let the cudgels prove who is the better man. (*To the Gipsy King.*)—There be good cudgels among you, I observe, lend us a set awhile, so that we may bring this folly to an issue.

SIR JOHN.—Agreed.

[*The cudgels are brought, a ring is formed, and* RAMORNIE *and* ROTHESAY *fight.* RAMORNIE *is disabled, and drops his cudgel; the Gipsies cheer; and* ROTHESAY *rushes forward and kisses the Gipsy girl.*

ROTHESAY.—Thus the better man wins the reward. So sweet is my reward, Maid Marion, that I would fain play another bout for a like courtesy. But after all, Sir John, I need not avow me the better man. If I have beaten thee, 'twas by a cunning turn yourself taught me, and in a moment more thy fate had likely been mine. Give me thy hand, I say, and forget this amicable love-strife of ours. What! you refuse? Think once again, friend of mine, before you refuse the hand of Rothesay. Well, well, there, your countenance lightens like the face of day after the passing of a thunder-cloud, and we are friends again. (*They shake hands.*) And now for a cup of good liquor for these good folks. Within, ho! Come hither, host, I say.

Enter HOST.

Here, John Tapster, take this fair company within, give them fair entertainment, feed them with your best, and give them to drink of your best. Give them wine, or mighty ale, or a cautious cup of stronger ware, if any there be among them who desire such; but treat them generously, John, and at mine expense; and mayhap I shall join the entertainment anon.

HOST.—Ay, ay, your Grace, I'se do your bidding with alacrity, for saving the occasion of a visit from your royal self, there is little stirring here in the way of business for an honest man.

ROTHESAY.—And yet you thrive, mine Host, and you are an honest man.

HOST.—True! but 'tis different now. God save our good King Robert, but he is a lameter and no sportsman; and the Falconland is deserted by him, totally deserted. Then our Duke Albany likes better to rule men, than to chase the deer in Falkland Park or to hunt down the wolf on the Lomond side; and so he comes but seldom here, and when he does come, he shuts himself up with his retinue, and little comes my way. Ah, 'twas far different in the days of your forbears, young Sir, for when the King came to Falkland to hunt, he brought a train of nobles with him that filled the town, and my poor house to overflowing; and nothing was heard but the sound of the horn, and the hearty laugh, and the song, from morn to night, with the clink of the cup and the entertainment. But times may mend with the help of your Grace, I trow.

ROTHESAY.—Well, well, lead your company to the house, and do my bidding. Sir John, pray accompany them, and preside at their merry-making until I join you all.

SIR JOHN.—The more willingly, that I may testify how completely my vapours have vanished. Now strike up music, and to the Inn, good folks, to the Inn, and there shall we carouse to the health of Scotland's Prince,—the sprightliest Prince in Christendom, the most accomplished and the best.

[*Music, and they enter the Inn.*

ROTHESAY [*Alone*].—I like not his tone; I like not his words. What! can Ramornie have begun to hate me? There was a flash in his eye, and a frown on his face, e'en now, that I marked with amazement, and love not when coupled with gentle words. Tut! I am foolish; he is my closest friend, and a momentary pique at his defeat in a paltry frolic can take no lasting hold on his heart. He is my elder,—true! I used to follow his lead closely,—true! And he likes to lead, and he enjoyed leading the Prince of Scotland. Now I know him for my inferior, and he knows it as well. True; but then he is large-hearted and generous. We have hawked together, hunted together, travelled together, wandered the wilds together; have slept side by side, and exchanged the vows of never-dying friendship. He cannot forget the past. No! Although I love to torment him, yet I love him as David loved Jonathan; and never shall I deem him mine enemy unless I have proof of his hostility. Even were he mine enemy, why, I am strong enough to look after myself, and to face him—and the devil at his back, an' he will. But see—

Enter CATHERINE GRAEME, *disguised as a Groom.*

Sweet Kate, would you have me chide? Why, you have kept Scotland's Regent waiting your coming! In truth, I began to fear you had decided to remain at home.

CATHERINE.—I have come, but am half-hearted in this business, and I sought you a short time agone to tell you so, but was unable to obtain speech of you. Oh, must I go? What shall the honest townsfolk say when they find I have fled with Duke Rothesay? Oh, my lord, my lord! I would you had never crossed my path! And yet, such is your influence over me, that you mould me like wax, and I *must* do your bidding! Even yet, allow me to turn back, I pray. I am unobserved, and no harm will be done were I to steal back gently to my home.

ROTHESAY.—And is it for this, Kate, that I have deserted the sister of Lindsay of Rossie?—the fairest maid, saving thyself, in the kingdom of Fife. Is it for this that I have contrived secret meetings with thee? and believed thy declaration that thou lovest me?—and so utterly, that thou wouldest do my bidding, go where I go, and dwell where I dwell? Be it so, Kate; return to thy home. I'll have no lukewarm love from thee, or any woman,—and so, farewell!

CATHERINE.—Oh, stay! let us not part thus. You know how friendless I am, how unprotected. Sad it is for a girl to dwell retired and aweary; and if your image fills my soul by night and by day, wherein am I in fault? Yes, Rothesay, let the world censure as it will, I'll follow thee, confiding my future, my all, to thy care and discretion. Thou hast vowed to cherish and protect me, and to wed me if the law allows. Oh, my lord, my lord! I do believe thy promise; and in token, here is my hand. I go with thee.

ROTHESAY.—Well said, Kate! My horses await us at the foot of the Castle Green; let us put foot in stirrup, and away,—away through the oaks of Falkland Park, and never shall we draw bridle until we reach the banks of the broad-bosomed Tay. And so, adieu to Falkland for the present. I'll make thee a lady, Kate, and thou shalt return here anon, in such bravery that thou shalt be the admiration of every man and the envy of every woman throughout the length and breadth of the kingdom of Fife.

[Exeunt.

SCENE III.—*A Room in Edinburgh Castle.* KING ROBERT *and* QUEEN ANNABELLA, ALBANY *and* RAMORNIE.

KING.—You tell me, Albany, the Prince hath fled?
ALBANY.—He came to Falkland, and declined to pass
    The portals of my stronghold. In the town
    He dwelt with an unruly company,
    Strollers and gipsies, thieves and vagabonds;
    And in the end he from that place eloped
    With a young damsel of the common folks.
    But whither they be gone, I cannot tell;
    Yet there's a murmur and a discontent
    Among the lieges at this freak of his
    I relish not, and gladly would allay.

QUEEN.—Alas, the reckless boy!   Yet, Albany,
    You clothe your meaning in ill-sorted garb,—
    The Prince of Scotland leagues him not with thieves.
    That he is foolish, well his mother knows,
    And careless of his rank, but never yet
    Did he degrade his state, or herd him with
    The vile and infamous.   I'll not believe it!

ALBANY.—Madam, you love your son ; and so, 'tis well.
    But hither have I brought his closest friend,
    Sore 'gainst his inclination, to attest
    What I advance.   Ramornie, do I lie?

SIR JOHN.—The Prince has led a merry life of late,—
    Yet wherefore question me?   I am his friend ;
    And hither was I brought, as you avowed,
    To tell their Majesties my humble mind
    Touching Duke Rothesay's future.

KING.—And hither have we come from the far west,
    From the retirement of our tranquil Bute,
    To weigh the future of our careless son.
    Alas, that ever he was born!   Alas,
    That I should grudge life to my eldest born,
    The scoff of Scotland, and his parents' shame!

QUEEN.—Nay, nay, my lord, have charity, have hope—
    Our son is young.   I've marked his qualities
    Since he was cradled ; though I must confess
    That he is reckless, rash, and arrogant,
    Yet there's an honesty of purpose in him,
    A winning gentleness, with dignity
    Combined, that gives me hope he yet will carve
    His name upon the frame of history
    By honourable deeds.   Hither we come,
    Confessing blame in him, but with the intent
    Of bettering his life.   Say now, Lord Duke,
    What would you with the youth?

ALBANY.—   Your Majesty
    Speaks to the point; were Rothesay mine own son,
    I'd bind him fast in matrimony's chains
    And tame his lusty spirit ; let him wed.

KING.—Will marriage tame him, brother?

ALBANY.—   Choose him a wife
    Modest and virtuous, high born and fair,
    Discreet and pure of soul,—my word on it,
    Her company will work a miracle
    Upon his restlessness.

QUEEN.—But is there such a maiden in our midst?

ALBANY.—The Earls of Douglas and of March are fain
    For an alliance with your royal house ;
    And each would with his daughter give a dower
    Proportioned to her rank.

KING.—   Hast seen these maidens?

ALBANY.—No ; but report would have it both are fair,
    And either is a prize for Scotland's Prince.
    It happens, too, that both are resident
    At this same present with the Lord of March.
    Say, shall I summon them to court ?
QUEEN.—Warily, warily, sir.   Why, know you not
    That to be won a maiden must be woo'd ?
    Hast seen the daughters of these lords, Sir John ?
SIR JOHN.—No ; but I learn that both are beautiful,—
    So beautiful, that Rothesay often vows
    He'll wander to their homes in quaint disguise
    To estimate their charms, himself unknown.
KING.—That you are Rothesay's friend, Duke Albany
    Proclaims you, sir.   Think you, were Rothesay wed,
    His levity of purpose were subdued ?
SIR JOHN.—Such is my firm opinion ; let him wed,
    And all is well.
KING.—We, too, have thought were Rothesay fitly mated,
    His kingly qualities would to the front.
    You know my son, young sir, have studied him,
    As Albany informs us, for his good ;
    Have watched his frolics with a guardian eye,
    And brought him safe from many a senseless broil.
    You love my son, are mentor, guardian, friend
    Combined, say, is it so ?
SIR JOHN.—   I love the Prince
    As if he were my younger brother, sir.
KING.—Then to Dunbar shall you proceed anon,
    To interview in our behalf and stead
    The maids of March and Douglas ; study well
    Their graces, gait, complexions, and the like.
    I warrant you are apt, Sir John, but more,
    Study their qualities of heart and mind,
    And in all candour then report to us
    If either be fit bride for Scotland's heir.
QUEEN.—Ay, more ; if both be queenly, we expect
    You shall pronounce in favour of the maid
    Best suited for our son in temp'rament
    And force of character.   You know him well ;
    Then study close, and relatively mark
    The dispositions of those highborn maids,
    For much depends on your report and choice.
SIR JOHN.—Much am I honoured in my mission, madam ;
    And I, the ambassador of love, shall aim
    To gain applause and credit, not alone
    From Scotland's Majesties, but from their son,
    Whose delegate as well as yours I'll be.
KING.—Well spoken, sir.   Duke Albany shall see
    That your equipment is prepared ; let all
    Be rich and suitable, as best beseems

The delegate of royalty.   For me !
I pray to God that Scotland's Prince, my son,
May marry one with virtue, intellect,
And power to guide her youthful lord aright.
For me ! I am a feeble broken man ;
I weary of this world, its foolishness,
Its sins, its broils and conflicts ; and would fain
Withdraw from earthly troubles, were my son
But fitted to encounter statesmanship.
But he is careless, and his government
Makes sport of royalty.   Ay, marriage, marriage,
'Tis the best cure for folly.   May this step
Lead him to honour, and myself to peace.
Farewell, good sirs, with all convenient speed
Arrange this mission.
QUEEN.—   Carry greetings, sir,
To one and all from Scotland's Majesty.
Be wary, most discreet, and politic,
For delicate your mission ; act it so
As to conciliate and not offend,
You thus shall gain our thanks and confidence.
And now, adieu !

                              [*Exeunt King and Queen.*

ALBANY.—Ramornie !
SIR JOHN.—I wait your question, sir.
ALBANY.—You love the Prince ?
SIR JOHN.—Surely, surely, when royalty decends
         To such as me, and deigns to term me *friend*,
         Then am I grateful, sir.
ALBANY.—Once more, Ramornie !
SIR JOHN.—The question, royal Duke ?
ALBANY.—You hate the Prince ?
SIR JOHN.—Hatred is mixed in quality, and I
         May not define the word, nor analyse
         The feeling.   What is hate ?
ALBANY.—When John Ramornie is carressed one hour,
         And spurned the next ; when he is smiled upon
         To-day, and frowned upon to-morrow ; when
         He finds him worsted by a younger man
         In games of skill, in fence, in love, in all
         That makes life worth possession ; all the while
         Being well aware that in the game of life
         He is this man's superior per force
         Of intellect ; why then, Ramornie *hates*,
         Can analyse hate in its subtlest sense,
         And is well able to define the word.
         A truce to quibbles, sir, you hate the Prince,
         And so do I ; 'twixt you and me have passed
         Hints of this common feeling ; now, 'tis time
         To speak together plainly, to conjoin

       Our thoughts inimical with one intent,—
       The overthrow of this imperious youth.
SIR JOHN.—Duke Albany, if one so near akin
       To Scotland's royalty confess thus far,
       Then may my humble self confess in turn
       That Rothesay holds light share of my regard.
ALBANY.—Spoken with caution, yet enough for me.
       You know that I was Scotland's governor
       Until this youth displaced me, at the will
       Of his fond mother and his doting sire.
       And since his elevation, well you know
       How he has lorded it upon my fall;
       Has gibed me, mocked me, sneered and scoffed at me
       Before the lords whom I was wont to rule
       With iron hand. Why, his lieutenancy
       He bears so lightly and so gaily, too,
       That rule with him is only sport and frolic.
       We must an end of this, and with your aid
       I'll so immesh him, that he'll wear the coils
       Of my contriving to his bitter end.
SIR JOHN.—I cannot aid ; my place is humble, sir.
ALBANY.—Listen.   His parents would a mate for him,
       And from their scheme I'll make me capital.
       Depart, I pray thee, on this embassage
       With all convenience, but so manage it
       That you embroil the Prince with one and all,
       Parents and daughters. Be it so contrived
       That you offend the families of March
       And Douglas both, and leave the rest to me.
       I'll rouse the factions into discontent,
       Till civil war ensue ; and in the crash
       Will Rothesay tumble down, to rise no more !
SIR JOHN.—My hatred's flame can never leap so high.
       There is no motive adequate to rouse
       My wrath to such an act of treachery.
ALBANY.—Tush ! I supply the motive ; set me firm
       In the viceregal chair, and gratitude
       Shall place you high among our proudest peers.
       You understand me?   Intellect and wit
       Are yours, but you are young ; so have a heed
       That you fulfil your mission to the letter,
       Nor let your heart betray your head.   Adieu!
       We will confer again upon your mission
       And my design, before you visit March.   *[Exit Albany.*
SIR JOHN.—I'll do your bidding, wily Albany,
       That on your shoulders I may raise myself
       To power and greatness.   When I look around,
       I see my fellow-man pursue one aim
       With never-swerving purpose, and that aim
       Is self ; and therefore, in this thing I do

I only run along the beaten track,
With this incentive,—hatred spurs me on.
For Rothesay, with his careless winning ways,
His easy grace and supercilious power,
His consciousness of my infe.ior place,
His taunting tongue, his scarce concealéd pride,
His thinly veiléd insults,—curse them all,—
Hath roused me to a hatred so intense
That, but to humble him, I'd risk good fame,
And bargain to my loss.　　But Albany
Will place a hidden weapon in my hand
Wherewith I strike ; if deadly be the blow,
Then Albany, not I, directs it so.　　　　　　　　　　　[*Exit.*

ACT II.

SCENE I.—*A Grove near Dunbar Castle.*

Enter ELIZABETH of DUNBAR *and* ELIZABETH DOUGLAS.

E. DUNBAR.—Sweet friend, or sister, rather, let me term thee,
　　For we are sisters in affection,—say,
　　What thinkest thou of this right-royal news
　　We have received to-day?
E. DOUGLAS.—　　　　　　　　　　I understand
　　His Majesty, whose feebleness prevents
　　His personal attendance, delegates
　　A visitor to March, Sir John Ramornie,
　　Who bears assurance of the kingly love
　　Towards his noble subject.
E. DUNBAR.—　　　　　　　　　　Empty show !
　　There's strategy with courtesy combined
　　In this unwonted mission.　 I have seen
　　But now the esquire of Ramornie,—he
　　Rode hither in hot haste to tell the Earl
　　His embassage (if I may term it so)
　　Approaches rapidly,—and in my ear
　　My father whispered that the mission's purpose
　　Is to obtain a bride for Scotland's Prince.
E. DOUGLAS.—And I may greet thee Scotland's future Queen !
E. DUNBAR.—Hush ! shall the daughter of Dunbar be bought
　　By King's commissioner?　 Not I, forsooth !
　　Am I a slave, that I am treated so?
　　Is this Ramornie to appraise my form,
　　To dwell upon the colour of mine eyes,

To note the texture of my hair, to mark·
My features and complexion, to applaud
Or disapprove my voice? I'll none of it ;
And he who would aspire to hand of mine,
Must woo in person. Shall I stand apart,
Shrinking and modest, while this delegate
Takes stock and invent'ry of this, my person,
For due report to Scotland's Majesties?
And shall I gaze beseechingly on him,
Imploring with mine eyes' mute eloquence
His good opinion? No, I tell you, no !
When he begins to fashion his report,
I'll deal the knave a buffet will astound him,
And to the King his master send him back,
A wiser and a more reflective man
Than when he sought Dunbar.

E. DOUGLAS.—   Have patience, sister,
The King is sickly, cannot ride abroad,
Else had he come in person to thy father.
That he has heard that thou art beautiful
I well believe. Nor is the King to blame
That thou hast beauty, birth, accomplishments,
Which do commend thee for his royal heir.
If thou art heart-free, sister, wherefore fret
At this unwonted honour to thy house,
And to thyself? This high commissioner
Comes hither but to summon thee to Court,
To good Queen Annabella. Where's the fault ?
I do confess, most of our Scottish maids
Would cry a welcome to Ramornie's mission.

E. DUNBAR.—Sweet sister, ofttimes I have envied thee
Thy face, the home of modesty and love ;
And I do envy thee thy gentleness
And meekness, that control my haughty thoughts
When they would wreck me. Let this delegate
Arrive, all-conscious of his king's behest.
I shall receive him honourably ; more,
I shall, when fit occasion serves, propose
Thyself as fitting bride for the young Prince.
Thou art a Douglas, and the Douglas blood
Ranks with the Stewart's. Thou art beautiful,
More beautiful than I. Say but the word,
For very friendship I'll transfer to thee
My influence, so that thou wed this Prince !
Nay, look not sad ; I do but jest, and vow
That neither king, nor prince, nor delegate
Shall ever cross the current of our loves ;
But while we live, Elizabeth of March
Shall be thy sister and unswerving friend !
But see ! who comes? 'tis but Ramornie's esquire.

Enter ROTHESAY, *attired as an Esquire.*

ROTHESAY.—I crave your pardon, noble ladies, I
    Await the coming of my chief, and fain
    To view the beauties of this famous spot
    Have wandered hither; I shall now withdraw.

E. DOUGLAS.—A well-graced youth; alas, how pale he looks !
    Address him softly.   [*Aside to* E. DUNBAR.

E. DUNBAR.—   Welcome to Dunbar.
    Sir John Ramornie's esquire, art thou not?
    For I was with my father, and beheld
    Thy coming hither.

ROTHESAY.—   Then I do address
    Lady Elizabeth, Lord March's daughter?
    I thank thee, lady, for thy courtesy.

E. DUNBAR.—You come from Court, how goes it with the King?

ROTHESAY.—Indiff'rent well, his ailments gain on him,
    I grieve to say.

E. DUNBAR.—   Her Majesty the Queen?

ROTHESAY.—Alas ! there's in the face of our good Queen
    A look I love not; care lays hold on her.
    Her form, once lithe and active, seems to droop
    As she were held of sickness.   God preserve her !

E. DOUGLAS.—The lad has tenderness of heart; his tones
    Ring gentleness, as if her Majesty
    Were mother to him.   [*Aside.*

E. DUNBAR—And young Duke Rothesay, Governor of Scotland,
    How fares it with him and his government?

ROTHESAY.—The Prince is well, for recently I saw him.
    But, lady, I am humble, nor aspire
    To question how the Lord Lieutenant rules.

E. DUNBAR.—Well said; you are a courtier.   We have heard
    The Prince is careless in his government,
    But, let that pass, can'st thou describe him to us,
    His face, his form? is he a proper man?
    Describe him pri'thee.

ROTHESAY.—Lady, I cannot well describe a man.
    A maiden's charms I love to dwell upon,
    And I describe the sex indiff'rent well.
    As for the Prince, I dare a parallel,—
    My humble self is not unlike to him
    In face and figure, so 'tis said at Court;
    And that Duke Rothesay is a proper man
    Has never been denied.

E. DUNBAR.—   Audacious youth !
    You tell me you can well describe the sex;
    Give us a sample of thy boasted art,—
    Describe us twain before you.

E. DOUGLAS.—   Halt, I pray;
    You bring the vivid blush upon his cheek,
    You press him overmuch.

ROTHESAY.— Impossible
For my poor tongue to syllable the praise
Of what's beyond all praise.

E. DUNBAR.— How mean you, sir?

ROTHESAY.—I stand in presence of perfection, ladies ;
A comprehensive word,—I can no more.

E. DUNBAR.—The tresses of my sister here are fair,
While mine are dark as night ; how can both be
Perfection, when both differ?

ROTHESAY.— Yet the rose
Is perfect in its way, so is the lily.

E. DUNBAR.—And you prefer the lily to the rose?

ROTHESAY.—I said not so ; the rose is queen of flowers.

E. DUNBAR.—And the fair lily?

ROTHESAY.— Empress, to my mind.

E. DUNBAR.—Now have I caught thee tripping, for the lily
Is modesty's design ; thou dost bestow
Misnomer on the lily, gentle sir.

ROTHESAY.—Then let me term the lily "Queen of flowers"
If so it please you,—"Empress" be the rose.
Both are perfection of their different kind.

E. DOUGLAS—See, on this grassy knoll the harebell grows,—
I better love to name it the bluebell,—
A humble flower, yet passing beautiful
And worthy of a Scottish maiden's wear.
I pluck the flower, I place it in thy hand ;
Give it to her you think it suits the best.

ROTHESAY.—Thou art thyself a type of Scotland's fairest,
For Scotland's fairest are blue-eyed ; but yet,
This flower has bloomed upon the soil of March,—
The daughter of Lord March shall·wear the flower.

E. DUNBAR—What ! Get thee gone, thou malapert, thou knave ;
Thou art saucy, lad. That foolish tongue of thine
May bring thee mischief; get thee gone, I say,
And learn discretion at thy mother's knee.
How ! art thou rooted to the spot? Begone,
Else, woman as I am, I'll lay my hands
Upon thee lustily. [*She advances threateningly towards*
ROTHESAY, *who stands firm.*

ROTHESAY.— Ha ! darest thou——

E. DUNBAR.—Dare ! by the spirit of mine ancestress,
Wild Agnes of Dunbar——

ROTHESAY.— Enough ! No more !
Black Agnes was an honour to our land ;
She shewed the spirit of a man when war
Aroused her blood, but in the hour of peace
She cultivated hospitality,
Nor spurned the stranger from her castle gates.

E DUNBAR.—'Tis true, young sir ; you have reminded me
You are my father's visitor. 'Tis well,

You shall be honoured in that circumstance ;
But never bandy words again with one
Who is entreated with all courtesy
(As is her due) by all within these bounds,
Nor tempt the flight of lofty rhetoric
If you would shun a fall.   Your years are few,
You are a very fledgling in the art
Of flattery, and needs must plume your wing
Before you soar with proper strength and grace.
Come, sister, leave him to his meditation.

> [*Exeunt, and* ROTHESAY *stands motionless,*
> *gazing on the ground.*

Re-enter ELIZABETH DOUGLAS.

E. DOUGLAS.—Poor youth, his pride is wounded ; motionless
He stands, with knitted brows and pallid face.
My heart is strangely stirred ; it cannot be
That I am interested in this boy
(For very boy he is, or little more).
There stands he, slim of figure, delicate
Of feature, proud of aspect, beautiful !
What ! dare I make confession to myself
That he, a stranger to mine eyes till now
Is comely ?   Read thy heart, Elizabeth,
And quickly summon up the Douglas pride
To teach thee what is due the Douglas blood.
What is this youth to me ?   Nothing, O nothing !
Let me withdraw, he has observed me not,
And yet,—O heart of mine, but thou art heavy
As lead within my bosom,—till this day
I might not lay my hand upon my heart
To still its heaviness ; for until now
I knew not that my heart could bear a load
Like this that vexes me.   I shall withdraw—
No ! I shall stay one moment.   Listen, sir ;
A single word ere I rejoin my friend.
Give me these bluebells,—what ! hast thou forgot them ?
There,—I shall carry them upon my breast
Until they fade ; and may thine anger die
Long ere their bloom expires.   Now, fare thee well.   [*Exit.*

ROTHESAY.—Not *fare thee well !* we meet again ere long,
And through thine agency, O gentle maid,
I'll read the daughter of Dunbar a lesson
Will serve her for a lifetime.   Let me hence
To meet Ramornie, and encounter him
With fair excuses for my presence here ;
For I, a royal, though unbidden guest
Do mar his embassy.   My honoured father,
'Twas like thyself to choose a bride for me
By deputy ; may I confirm the choice.

A she-wolf, and a maid? I'll wed the maid,
And tame the she-wolf to my heart's content.   [*Exit.*

SCENE II.—*A room in Dunbar Castle*, ELIZABETH OF DUNBAR *alone.*

E. DUNBAR.—He dared me to my face, this unknown lad;
And for his pains would I have struck him down
Had I but dared. 'Tis strange; this quality
Of courage in a stranger quells my wrath,
Bids me respect him, and remember him
To his advantage. Daughter of Dunbar,
Art thou turned weakling at a haughty glance?
Yet never did I meet a prouder eye
Than his; like a live coal it sudden gleamed
In undisguiséd wrath. I stood disarmed;
And since that moment I have thought on him,
And him alone. Now let me analyze
My truant thought. What is't possesses me?
Wrath? Nay,—I honour him for his defiance.
Hate? Nay,—I cannot hate where I respect.
Contempt? I may not hold him in contempt,
In that he is a youth; and for his birth,
He may be noble; there's that in his mein
Proclaims him noble. Tush! enow of this,
I'll think of him no more. When next we meet
Let me bespeak him gently. Yet, 'tis strange
I'deign to think upon a stranger thus.
I'll crush his pride ere I have done with him,
And bring him to his knees ere he depart
Th' inhospitable Castle of Dunbar!   [*Exit.*

SCENE III.—*The Great Hall in Dunbar Castle. Music. Enter
Gentlemen of the Household; then the* EARL OF MARCH, *leading
his Daughter* ELIZABETH; *with her* ELIZABETH DOUGLAS;
*then follow Attendants and Retainers. The Earl and Ladies
are stationed at the upper end of the Hall. Flourish, and
enter* SIR JOHN RAMORNIE, *with* SIR WILLIAM LINDSAY *and*
DUKE ROTHESAY *as his Esquires, then* RAMORNIE'S *Retinue.*

MARCH.—Sir John Ramornie, welcome to our halls;
Welcome to you and this good company.
That you, a courtly gentleman, have deigned
To honour my poor house, rejoiceth me,—
The more that you are held in high respect
For able counsel, probity, and worth
Among the governors of our fair realm;
Ramornie's name grows famous in the State.

SIR JOHN.—Thanks, my good lord. Your welcome I accept,
    Not for myself,—though you do flatter me,
    The humble statesman,—but as delegate
    Of good King Robert, whom God long preserve.
    The ailments of His Majesty increase ;
    His walk grows heavier, his strength declines,
    So that he cannot now proceed abroad
    With that alacrity his youth conferred.
    And yet, his royal interest never flags
    In kingdom, subjects, government, and law ;
    And on those subjects nearest to his throne,
    And dearest to his heart, would he bestow
    The signal honour of a royal visit,
    Did but his strength allow ; but failing this,
    His Majesty laid his commands on me,
    His delegate and representative,
    To visit you, my lord, and give expression
    Of his contentment in your loyalty.
    Here are my letters of commission, sir,
    Under the King's sign-manual.
MARCH.—   I accept
    These letters with all rev'rence.   As for you,
    With all respect shall we entreat you, sir,—
    Firstly, as royal delegate ; and, next,
    As gentleman of most approvéd merit.
    Somewhat I learn of this your mission from
    This youthful esquire stationed on your right,
    Who, as you are aware, rode in advance
    To herald your approach.   Give us his name,
    For in the hurry of his tidings I
    Have lacked in courtesy.
E. DUNBAR [*Aside*].—Now shall I learn his name and his degree ;
    If he be noble, I can smile on him.
E. DOUGLAS [*Aside*].—Now stay thy throbbing, foolish heart of
        mine ;
    Whether he's noble, or of low degree,
    Yet there he standeth, nature's nobleman !
SIR JOHN.—His name is David.
MARCH.—And his title is ?
SIR JOHN.—The Lord of Lomond-side.
MARCH.—From Stirling's walls
    Have I beheld Ben Lomond's haughty crest.
SIR JOHN.—The Lomond that entitles him uprears
    Her lowlier head in Fife.
ROTHESAY.—No more, I pray thee.
    My Lord of March, let me declare myself.
    I am Duke Rothesay ; hither have I come
    Auxiliar to Ramornie and his mission.
    And therein pardon me my heedlessness,
    My boldness, my presumption, in that I

Have crossed your threshold an unbidden guest.
Ramornie knew not of my coming hither,—
Frown not, Sir John ; my father's delegate
Lords it supreme above my father's son,
And therein stands your mission here intact,—
But he will pardon me, when I confess
That I regret I communed not with him
Ere I resolved on this unwonted step.
My lord, upon your hospitality,
Far-famed and generous, I throw myself ;
Say, am I welcome here ?

MARCH.—Thrice welcome, noble Rothesay ; let this day
Be ever honoured by the house of March.

ROTHESAY.—But not your hospitality alone
Advised me hither. I have heard, my lord,
The daughter of the noble house of March
Outshines in beauty Scotland's fairest fair,
And 'tis my duty as a courtly knight
To lay upon the altar of her charms
The incense of my admiration. But
' I stand perplexed. Have you two daughters, sir ?

MARCH.—Here stands Elizabeth of March, and here
Elizabeth of Douglas.

ROTHESAY [*To Elizabeth of March*].—Rumour, O lady, dubbed
thee beautiful ;
But Rumour's thousand tongues were all too few
To tell, and justly tell, thy countless charms.
[*To Elizabeth Douglas.*
And all by contrast art thou beautiful
Exceedingly. That both are bosom friends
Have I been told. Doubtless the one exults
And glories in the other's loveliness.

E. DUNBAR.—Sir, you have said your say ; and passing well
The words trip off your tongue. 'Tis now my turn.
Know, then, I love no smoothly-spoken man,
With flattery like to honey on his lips.
I am the daughter of a warlike race,
And love to hear a man speak like a man,
Without the lisp of self-conceited youth,
But boldly to the point, with ne'er a turn
Of art to soothe the humour of a maid,
Or ply her vanity.

MARCH.—   Be quiet, girl ;
You know not what you say. Your temper twists
Your manners out of joint.

E. DUNBAR.—And I stand here, forsooth, to be appraised
By this sweet-mannered, slender, beardless boy !
Go ! be a man before you speak to maids
Of beauty and their charms.

MARCH.—   Pert lass, enough !

The Duke will in due time speak for himself
In other wise, I trow. Now, let us hence
Unto the banquet hall ; for you, Sir John,
And this good company, need food and rest
After your lengthy road. I lead the way ;
So follow, one and all. My royal guest
Shall lead my daughter to the banquet. You,
Sir John, shall lead her friend, Earl Douglas' daughter.
So ! all is well arranged. Now let us on.

  [*Music.* DUKE ROTHESAY *takes* RAMORNIE *by*
    the hand, and conducts him to ELIZABETH
    DUNBAR.

ROTHESAY.—Lady, behold the King's high delegate :
To him belongs the honour of your hand.
'Tis I am only Prince of Scotland ; I
Give place unto my sire, to Scotland's King ;
And with Earl Douglas' daughter shall I follow,
Provided she thus far shall honour me.

    [*Gives his hand to* ELIZABETH DOUGLAS.

E. DUNBAR. — Proud youth, I read your meaning. Scotland's
  Prince,
In absence of the King, might well aspire
To fill his father's room at such a time.
'Tis well ! You scorn me,—you refuse my hand ;
And offer, in well counterfeited meekness,
To follow me. This is my answer, sir,—
I take the hand of John Ramornie—thus—
And cast it from me with disdain. Away !
I'll none of Scotland's delegate, or thee !   [*Exit.*

MARCH.—Forgive her ; she is sore perplexed to-day
With this adventure. I shall reason with her,
And bid her crave your pardon on the morrow.

ROTHESAY.—Nay ! for her anger well becometh her,
And in her wrath she beams majestical,
So that I would not lose a gesture of her scorn
To gain her honied speech. Leave her to time,
And to herself ; her mood will change anon.
When fiercest blows the storm, we may expect
The earlier calm.—And now, my Lord of March,
On to the banquet hall. We follow thee.   [*Exeunt.*

———

SCENE IV.—*A Room in Edinburgh Castle*, DUKE ALBANY *alone*

ALBANY.—The crown ! what is the crown ? Oh, rebel thought
That from the lines of discipline will burst,
To war against my peace. The crown is power ;
And I, like other men born to the rule,

Exist for power, its triumphs, sweets, rewards,
And all that centres fame within one man.
Who stands between the crown and me?   The King,—
A feeble man, in mind and body weak,
And hasting to his grave.   He may be King
In title, yet I king it over him,
Were not this heir-apparent in the front,—
A saucy stripling, rude, unmannerly,
And conscious of his place.   With other men
I bear me hardily ; can beat them down
With angry word, or frown, or haughty glance.
But this lad baffles me.   He answers sneer
With doubled sneer ; he meets my glance of hate
With calm contempt ; he reads Duke Albany.
Well, let him read ; there's more inside the book
That comprehends my soul than he can read ;
For to my inner self stands unconfessed
The history that I shall write for him.
The royal pair would see young Rothesay wed,
To sober him, forsooth, for statesmanship !
That is, to shelve myself, who long did rule,
Lieutenant of the King.   If Rothesay wed,
And in the State becomes an active power,
Then I become a cipher, for this lad
Has brains and subtlety.   I'll none of this ;—
He shall not wed.   How stands it at this present?
The Lords of March and Douglas, anxious both
For royal honours, secretly advance
Their daughters' claims to be our future Queen ;
And to that end they bribe the King and me
(For bribe it is) with heavy sums of gold.
But Douglas bribes the highest.   Shall we then
Restore their bribe to the unwedded house?
Or to both houses, if this marriage scheme
Miscarry?   No!   The crown hath need of gold,—
And I have need of gold, for gold is power.
We keep the gifts, and leave the Prince unwed ;
And if the jealous, discontented lords
Enkindle war against their King, not I,
But Rothesay, has the fall.   How now?

Enter Sir WILLIAM LINDSAY.

LINDSAY.—   Your Grace,
   I come with private tidings from Dunbar.
ALBANY.—Ha !   Welcome, Rossie ; that you are my friend
   I know right well.   How goes it at Dunbar?
LINDSAY. — Bravely, your Grace.   You know Duke Rothesay's
      there ?
ALBANY.—Something of this I heard ; the wings of love
   Are ever ready for the lusty flight.

And I have heard that Rossie's shady groves
Were visited of Cupid and the Prince
Ere he betook him to Dunbar. Is 't so ?
LINDSAY.—My bitter curse upon young Rothesay's head !
'That he seduced my sister, you know well.
Had it not been so, I had not stood here
This day your willing spy, and bitter foe
To Scotland's heir. If you would use me, sir,
To work your enmity against the Prince,
Refrain from taunt or gibe, or heedless word
Upon a subject that nigh maddens me
When I reflect on't.
ALBANY.—   Pardon me, young sir.
'That you and yours have suffered grievous wrong
I know, nor shall I indiscreetly touch
Upon this topic further. Tell me, now,
How goes our mission to the Lord Dunbar?
LINDSAY.—That two Elizabeths are there you know,
The daughters of the Lords of March and Douglas.
Both are surpassing beautiful ;—the one
Dark as the night, the other fair as day ;—
A very wonder 'tis to gaze on both,
To doubt which is the lovelier. When the Prince
Arrived, i'faith, he scanty welcome had
From March's daughter. Like the gentle doves,
Their courtship 'gan in pecking and disdain ;
But now, they're closer drawn ; and, I am told,
Their scorn is turned to love.
ALBANY.—   Ha ! here are news.
And Douglas' daughter calmly stands aside,
Without a maiden effort on her part
To win the heir of Scotland?
LINDSAY.—   So it is.
Her modesty forbids her to enact
The part of lover.
ALBANY.—   Wonder among women !
Speak you to this of your own knowledge, sir?
LINDSAY.—Of my part knowledge, and the private word
Of John Ramornie.
ALBANY.—   Rossie, I do thank you
For this intelligence. I shall requite
This favour with another. Rest assured
The day will come, and soon, when you shall have
Full measure of revenge upon your foe ;
For on the news you bring shall your revenge
Have resting-place. And now retire, my friend,
But keep within convenient distance, for
His Majesty and I have need of you.
LINDSAY.—If the King's will be coupled with your own,
I'll do his bidding, and right cheerfully.   [*Exit.*

ALBANY.—So ! he would wed the daughter of Lord March !
    But Douglas is ambitious, and would mate
    His daughter with the Prince.   I'll spoil the game,
    And rouse an enmity between these lords
    Will kindle Scotland into civil war.   •
    First, I shall captivate the Douglas' pride
    With mention of my nephew's preference
    For his fair daughter ;—next, I'll send him on
    To March, to bear the damsel to her home,
    Betrothed of royalty.   Unless I lure
    The Douglas on by such-like specious note,
    Never would he approach his rival's halls.
    Then, when the explanation comes, 'twere sport
    To see his fury at his rival's glee !
    'Tis war between them !—war !—and to the knife.
    And next for March.   'Twere easy to delay
    A marriage with his daughter.   Hath not March
    Been niggard of his gifts compared with Douglas?
    And till the royal coffers be surcharged
    (And mine as well) with much increase of gold,
    March cannot hope to see his daughter wed
    To Scotland's heir.   A tangled skein is this ;—
    But in my hands I'll draw the thread so fine,
    That I shall ruin Rothesay with these lords,
    And with his feeble sire.   Mine is the game !
    And next, to oust from his lieutenantcy
    My haughty nephew.   Oh, I love him well !
    And he shall have due earnest of my love.   *[Exit.*

SCENE V.—*A Room in Dunbar Castle,* ELIZABETH OF DUNBAR *and*
                SIR JOHN RAMORNIE.

SIR JOHN.—   Hear me, lady.
E. DUNBAR.—You dare to speak of love !   You but insult
    My state.   Away !   You know me not.
SIR JOHN.—   ,   Alas !
    Methought that honest love insulted never.
E. DUNBAR.—You cannot say that yours is honest love.
    Here you remain, the Monarch's delegate
    To win me for his heir; and yet you plead
    Not for his heir, but for your simple self !
    You are dishonest in your embassy.
SIR JOHN.—Nay ! for the Prince is here in person ; he
    Can woo without mine aid.   My mission's done.
E. DUNBAR.—Your mission stands until you are discharged.
    Enough ! and know, Elizabeth of March
    Shall never, saving with an equal, wed.

SIR JOHN.—You aim at marriage with the Prince.   Ah's me!
  That I could touch your cold, ambitious heart.
  Wedded to thee, what could I not perform?
  I have ambition equal to thine own;
  And with thy lofty sp'rit to urge me on,
  Oh, I would reach the pinnacle of fame,
  And proudly share my glory with thyself.
E. DUNBAR.—It may not be; he who aspires to win
  This hand must be born great.   I love thee not.
SIR JOHN.—But I could teach thee readily to love
  As never woman loved before.
E. DUNBAR.—   O, fool!
  To prate of love, and to a woman, thus!
SIR JOHN.—You love the Prince, but know—he loves you not;
  His heart is given to Earl Douglas's daughter.
  Ha! you turn pale; your confidante, your friend,
  Keeps the sweet secret of her maiden love
  In the recesses of her bosom buried;
  And she can meet you daily, hourly, yet
  Contrive to blind you to her lofty aim—
  The hand of Scotland's Prince.   You know her not.
E. DUNBAR.—I know Elizabeth, and I know you.
  Learn, then, ambitious man, that from her lips
  Have I been warned against Ramornie's wiles.
  As you approach me now, her you approached
  With honied words, had woo'd her for your bride;
  But with disdain, nigh equal to mine own,
  (Though she be meek) she would have none of you.
  And now, forsooth, you, sir, would condescend
  To give me the reversion of your hand!
  Away! unprincipled, ambitious churl,
  Else will I bid my father drive you forth
  Despite the armour of your embassy.
SIR JOHN.—Lady, I go, and with this parting word,—
  I'll keep you ever in my memory.   [*Exit.*
E. DUNBAR.—Intrigue is written on that courtly face.
  Much I mistrust the man; yet is he vain,
  And shallow at the best, when he aspires
  To mate with Scotland's proudest.   Said I, *proudest?*
  Alas! where has my pride evanishéd?
  Since I have made acquaintance with this Prince,
  And learned to love him, all my pride is gone,
  And I am but a humble woman now,
  Prepared to sacrifice my haughtiness
  For Rothesay's love.   Yet, shall I give my heart
  To him who to another giveth his?
  'Tis false! for he loves me: his tones are soft,
  Like low sweet music, when he speaks to me;
  While in his eye there gleams a nameless light
  That only kindles at the torch of love.

And I, alas, am in love's trammels caught ;
Am tamed, and taught to sigh the hour away
That keeps young Rothesay from my side !   O, Love !
I who despised thee, bend the knee to thee,
And make confession of thy hidden power.
Whiles would I bid thee go, and give me peace,
For there's a heaviness that weights my heart
Early and late since thou mad'st lodgment here ;
But I remember that to banish thee
Kills pleasing pain, and makes existence void ;
Thus would I have thee stay ; but am I happy ?
Nay, miserable.   O ! what's this youth to me ?
He's naught to me.   Yet surely do I err,
For I do know he is my all in all,
My life, my paradise !   Ah, foolish heart,
How light thou grow'st when Rothesay's by my side ;
But in his absence thou art weighted down
As lead, and my sole occupation tends
To think on him, ponder his every word,
His accents, trick of talk, his grace of form,
His gait, and comeliness.   Enough of this,
Else will I in my weakness loathe myself.
Yet did Ramornie say he loves me not.
Now, by high heaven, if this be the truth,
There mixes with my love a jealousy
That would ordain me to a dire revenge
On him who hardily would dare to slight
The honour of my name !   Ah ! jealousy
Thou'rt kin to love, and yet love's enemy !
Who comes ?   The Prince !   with him, Elizabeth.
Now let me act a mean invidious part
To kill uneasiness, and learn the truth ;
I'll step behind the arras till they part.
                    [*She retires behind the arras.*

Enter ROTHESAY *and* ELIZABETH DOUGLAS.

E. DOUGLAS.—Trust not Ramornie, he is dangerous.
ROTHESAY.—He loves thee, and therein is dangerous
     To his own peace and mine.
E. DOUGLAS.—   Not to *thy* peace.
     Am I not thine for ever and for ever ?
     Then wherefore fear Ramornie ?
ROTHESAY.—   Ever since
     I first did make acquaintance with the man
     Have I been destined to oppose his aims
     Or thwart his projects.   My inferior he,
     In station, birth, and knightly exercise,—
     And sorely does he fret to know it so,—
     Hence is he dangerous.   He hates his friend,
     And friendship turned to hatred rivals hell.

He loved thee when he first cast eyes on thee ;
He loves thee now ; had fain persuaded me,
For his own purpose, ere he knew my love,
That thou wert all uusuited for my bride,
And that thy friend, the daughter of Lord March,
Was destined by my parents to be mine.
Nay, look not sad ; my royal parents choose
As Rothesay chooses.   What ! are not mine eyes
Mine own, and shall I gaze with borrowed light
Upon my future wife ?   Thou art my choice,
The sweetest, fairest maid in Christendom ;
And John Ramornie's welcome, an' he list,
To woo and wed the daughter of Dunbar.

E. Douglas.—Hear me, Duke Rothesay.

Rothesay.—   David is my name,
And sweet that name when syllabled by thee.

E. Douglas.—Yes, thou art David to my inmost soul,
But Rothesay to the world.   Doubt not my love,
For, O, it glorifies and animates
My spirit, and I only live for thee !
When thou art present, happiness, content,
And joy unspeakable are mine ; but when
Thou leav'st my side, the brightness of my sun
Is clouded o'er, and borrowed happiness
Is only mine by dwelling on thyself,
Thy glance, thy smile, and kingly qualities.
I cannot think of thee, my future lord,
As aught but perfect.   Yet, forgive me now
If I inquire, hast thou done right in this,—
To cause my friend, Elizabeth Dunbar,
To deem thy love was hers ?   Is it not so ?
Hast thou not whispered in her secret ear
That thou aspirest to her hand ?

Rothesay.—   'Tis true,
But yet I love her not.

E. Douglas.—   And yet, methinks,
Love's counterfeit was present in thine eyes
When thou didst speak to her.   Now, wherefore this ?

Rothesay.—'Twas in revenge that I have acted thus.
When hither first I came, she loaded me
With contumely and taunts, until for shame
I blushed before mine own inferiors,
And thereupon I vowed to be revenged.
This, this is my revenge, to cause her love me,
And waken to the truth—I love another !

E. Douglas.—Alas ! but thou hast done a grievous wrong
To my poor friend.   Weak is a woman's heart,
And slighted love is a sharp instrument
That pierces,—yes, it may be to the death.
Let me, I pray thee, undeceive my friend ;

I'll break the tidings to her gently, and
As woman best to woman can.   Alas !
That thou hast learned to love me, for 'tis true
Elizabeth Dunbar were fitter mate
For Scotland's Prince than I.

ROTHESAY.—No, thou art feminine : a vixen she,
A cat, a tigress rather, who would rule
Her husband and the realm with sharpset claws ;
But never shall she rule in realm of mine.
She has the spirit of her ancestress,
Black Agnes, and (they tell) her face and form.
Both were born rulers, with this difference,—
Black Agnes's love-shafts piercéd to the heart ;
Black Bess's love-shafts never piercéd mine.
I'll tell her this anon.   [*Enter* ELIZABETH DUNBAR, *suddenly.*

E. DUNBAR.—   She stands before thee,
She has heard *all ;* thy love and thy revenge.
Rothesay, I know thee now, and thank my God
That I have listened to the very truth
From thine own lips, for never else had I
Believed in the existence of a man
Self-villified as thou.   My passion died
As thou didst tell thine infamy !   I stand
Amazed to think that thou, a royal Prince,
Could'st calmly tell thy baseness, and to *her !*
O ! rare revenge to win a woman's heart
With hollow vows and protestations vain,
With the vile object to deride her love
And scoff at her affection !   Ha ! the blush
Of conscious shame reddens thy cheek at last.
No man that's worthy of the name could act
The part that thou hast done.   .

ROTHESAY.—I blush ! 'tis for thy shrewish tongue.   Thy love
Being gone, thy temper reasserts itself.

E. DUNBAR.—And thou, Elizabeth, my bosom friend,
My sweet companion, thou could'st stoop to this ?
Could'st meet me daily, hourly, smile on me,
And fawn on me, yet steal away his heart ?
There stands thy lover, art thou proud of him ?

E. DOUGLAS.—Reproach me not, for I have learned to love him.

E. DUNBAR.—Have we not been as sisters? more than sisters?
Had I a single thought concealed from thee ?
By day we parted not, and in the night
Have we not shared one couch, jealous, I trow,
Lest sleep might drown our close companionship
In still oblivion and requiréd rest?
Well didst thou know my soul's affection turned
Around this man, for I have told it thee
A thousand times, and in a thousand ways,
Yet never once by word or sign hast thou

Displayed thy passion for this perjured Prince.
Go, take thy lover. I despise you both ;
And may ye prosper as your loves deserve !

Enter the EARLS OF MARCH *and* DOUGLAS *with* SIR JOHN RAMORNIE

MARCH.—Daughter, art saucy? When thy voice is raised,
    Methinks a tempest's brewing.
DOUGLAS.—   I have come,
    Sweet lady mine, to see my daughter's friend
    In her own home. Has not Elizabeth
    A welcome word for me?
E. DUNBAR.—Welcome, my Lord.
DOUGLAS.—Thou hast done my bidding, lass, and welcomed me ;
    I ask no more, yet welcome spoken thus
    Freezes the soul of hospitality.
    Let me withdraw my daughter from this house,
    For if the sire be in this fashion treated
    The daughter may not longer tarry here.
MARCH.—Have patience, Douglas, I am master here ;
    I bid thee welcome. If thy coming be
    In courtesy to me, treat this my home
    And all therein as thine. As for my daughter,
    This amorous youth has turned her head, I trow,
    By dangling matrimony's golden bands
    Before her eyes. Ah ! saucy daughter mine,
    When thou hast left my home a royal bride
    Thy manners thou wilt mend ; there is no curb
    Like marriage for the temper.
DOUGLAS.—   On my life
    I understand thee not. Duke Rothesay, speak,
    What mystery is this? What ! silent, sir ?
    Know, my Lord March, it was Duke Albany
    Did notify to me that Scotland's Prince
    My daughter has betrothéd ; hither I
    After the announcement came, as her convoy
    To the metropolis, there to abide
    Until the marriage-day.
MARCH.—   Ha ! you soar high.
    Another royal marriage for the Douglas !
    Now, John Ramornie, by your knighthood speak,—
    Since you came here, our Monarch's delegate,
    To seek my daughter's hand for Scotland's Prince,
    Have you not whispered in my private ear
    That Rothesay was enamoured of my child,
    And that a delegate was needed not
    To prompt the courtship?
RAMORNIE.—Such was my belief.
ROTHESAY.—Silence, good Lords, and worthy delegate.
    That there was controversial matter here,
    I do admit. The controversy ends,

And in this wise,—here standeth my betrothed,
Elizabeth of Douglas.   Say, sweet Bess,   .
Art not my promised wife ?
E. DOUGLAS.—'Tis even so.
ROTHESAY.—And if Earl Douglas deigns to give his daughter,
   The fairest flower mine eyes e'er dwelt upon,
   Into my keeping, I will cherish her,
   And in all honour so maintain her state,
   That none occasion shall she ever have
   To rue she links her destiny to mine.
   Give her to me, my Lord.
DOUGLAS.—   I do consent,
   Elizabeth of Douglas shall be yours.
MARCH.—God's death ! but this is strange !   Ye brave it, sirs,
   As ye were in the Douglas Castle, not
   Our stronghold of Dunbar.   But have a care,
   Ere ye depart I 'll explanation have
   Of this discourtesy to me and mine.
   Ramornie, speak ! did not this royal youth
   (Or have mine eyes deceived me) pay true court
   To mine own daughter ?
RAMORNIE.—   So it was ;
   And my Duke Rothesay will admit the fact,
   That in all earnestness I counselled him
   To bring his wooing to a bearing, and
   Entreat betrothal.
MARCH.—And he answer gave ?
RAMORNIE.—That though I be King Robert's delegate,
   Yet in the choosing of a bride, himself
   Would act, but never I.
MARCH.—   Presumptuous lad,
   Self-willed and arrogant, you ventured here,
   And with the honour of a noble house
   Tampered, to pass the idle hour away ;
   I 'll reckon heavily with you for this.
   And my Lord Douglas, you too venture here,
   To treat the delegation of our King
   With thinly-veiled contempt, making pretence
   That you obey the King through Albany,
   And his foul stratagems.   I see it all !
   'Tis Albany against his Sovereign set,
   With Rothesay for a cat's paw.   I proclaim
   You wholly false, wholly ambitious,
   An evil counsellor, an evil friend ;
   A grasping subject, whom the very throne
   Would barely serve for your ambition.   Sir,
   Depart these walls, else will I break the laws
   Of hospitality, and on this spot
   Hold reckoning for your duplicity.

DOUGLAS.—Ha! you defy the Douglas! On the word,
　　Base lord, I answer your defiance thus—
　　　　　　　　[DOUGLAS *and* MARCH *draw*, ELIZABETH
　　　　　　　　　OF MARCH *steps between them.*
E. DUNBAR.—Put up your swords, and leave this cause to me;
　　Herein have I concern. Ramornie, answer!
　　Not for the King alone, but for his son
　　You acted delegate, in that you whispered
　　Often and often, in my private ear,
　　That he did love me,—this you will confess?
RAMORNIE.—I had authority for this; the Prince
　　Did so declare.
E. DUNBAR.—Little experience have I had in love,
　　Yet woman's wit is quick, and I have noted
　　That you aspired to that fair lady's hand.
　　Start not, Lord Douglas, with your haughty house
　　Had this ambitious schemer leagued himself.
　　Say thou, Elizabeth, did not this man
　　Ask thee in marriage? See! no answer, lords;
　　Her very silence answers me and you.
　　Ramornie, you have dared to love this maid,
　　And thought to shield her from Duke Rothesay's love
　　(Altho' until this day I knew it not)
　　By mating him with me. Hence your poor wiles,
　　Your artifice, devices, trickery,
　　And sugared messages sent to and fro!
　　But all without avail, for from the sum
　　And reckoning you left young Cupid out,
　　And he has baffled you. Next, when you saw
　　That you were powerless to prevent their loves,
　　You dared to cast your eyes upon myself.
　　Nay, father, start not, he did honour me,
　　This delegate of royalty, whose scheme
　　Miscarried,—he did honour me, ay me,
　　With tender of his hand! But I declined,
　　In all respect,—be it said, in all respect,—
　　The destiny he had in store for me.
RAMORNIE.—Your heart, poor lady, was not yours to give;
　　You love Duke Rothesay.
D. DUNBAR.—　　　　　　　　But *you* love *me* not,
　　And yet had destined me to be the prop
　　And ladder to your greatness. True it is
　　I listened to Duke Rothesay, while I thought
　　He was sincere, for he did vow he loved me.
　　But accident—foe to duplicity—
　　Proclaims the Prince's falsity to me,
　　And from my conciousness I cast him off,
　　And scorn that ever I did bend on him
　　Affection's glance. No, sir, think not I love him,
　　The daughter of Lord March can never love

Where she remains unloved.   Enough of this ;
Hear me, good father, hear me, one and all
One moment more, to sum this matter up :—
Ramornie, you are foiled, depart in peace,
And learn the art of statecraft ; learn true love,
Ere on a delegation such as this
You venture forth again.   Duke Rothesay, take
Your blushing bride to the metropolis,
And guide her tenderly ; she was my friend,
Unuséd to deceit till she knew *you*.
Earl Douglas, with your daughter hie to Court,
And give your pride the rein, without one thought
For your poor daughter's after happiness.
And you, my father, bid your guests depart,
As 'tis best fitting them, in courtesy ;
Think not your daughter grieves the sorry day
That sees the heir to Scotland pass her by.
She knows him now, and now she knows herself ;
And in the knowledge, may she strive to be
A better and a milder-mannered maid
Than heretofore.   The world is wisdom's school,
And wisdom may be taught e'en by a fool.   [*Exeunt.*

ACT III.

SCENE I.—*A Room in Edinburgh Castle.*   KING ROBERT *and*
DUKE ALBANY.

KING.—Brother, can this be true?
ALBANY.—   I grieve to tell it,
    Yet true it is, Duke Rothesay's marriage vows
    Bind him not to good conduct.   For a time
    The world went smoothly with the wedded pair,
    And o'er his bride the ardent lover hung
    Enamoured of her charms ; satiety
    Succeeded, and he 'gan to treat his wife
    To frowns and taunts ; next, cold indifference
    Possessed him, and to win her husband back
    She strove, poor girl, with all the art she had
    To keep him by her side.   But wreathéd smiles
    And gentle words, and loving tenderness,
    Were all in vain.   He has deserted her ;
    And in the company of light-o'-loves
    He wiles the time away.
KING.—   Unhappy son of an unhappy sire !
    O that my Queen were only living now,
    To point to those unfortunates the way,
    With footsteps wary and discreet, to wend

Life's journey; but she's dead, alas, she's dead,
And I am left alone. Brother, you know
How frail I am, and sometimes I do think
This feeble temple of the soul, this frame,
Weakens my spirit, and I grow aweary
Of life and all life's burdens. Would to God
My son were noble-natured, chaste of heart,
And firm of government, how gladly I
Would cast my crown and royal state aside,
And bid him king it in this warlike land.
But I misdoubt him; and the line of Bruce
Myself shall represent until the day
That sees him cast frivolity aside,
And plume his manhood with his royalty.
Where is he now?

ALABNY.—'Tis thought he is in Fife.

KING.— Lindsay of Rossie
Is his sworn enemy. Harm may befal
My foolish son if he's at large in Fife.

ALBANY.—In Fife or out of Fife, I fear, good brother,
He's equally in danger. His the art
Or the misfortune (term it as we will)
To raise and to create new enemies,
By arrogancy and misgovernment,
With every passing hour. The Douglases,
The mightiest house in Scotland next the crown,
Vow vengeance on him for the Princess' sake,
The hapless daughter of their chief; Lord March
Is alienate, and utterly; the Graemes,
The Murrays, Crichtons, and a hundred more
Of Scotland's noblest, all cry shame on him
For his licentiousness and levity.
And if your Majesty continues him
In his lieutenancy, much do I fear
Rebellion will uprear her hydra head
Against your royal line; and all in vain
Your kingly influence to hold the Crown.

KING.—Something of this I feared. Advise me, brother,
For my son David's sake, and for mine own.
What shall I do?

ALBANY.—Depose your son from his lieutenancy.
By one bold stroke shall you assert yourself
And satisfy the people.

KING.— But my son,
Is he to abdicate his statecraft thus
For ever? That he has good parts I know,
And good ability. He condescends,
When in the mood, to such effect that all
Are captive. Then his lieutenancy
Is good apprenticeship to government,—

And he is Scotland's heir. If I depose him,
I care not to resume the reins of power;
For I am feeble, and my Queen is dead.
She, ever ready with a shrewd advice
To tread my difficulties under foot,
When I lost her, my strength of purpose died,
And here I droop and pine, and wonder much
That Providence created me a king;   '
For who so unambitious as myself,
Or more unfitted to uphold a throne?
ALBANY.—Brother, your grief bids you decry yourself.
The people love King Robert; 'gainst the son
They clamour, not the father.
KING.—   Who shall rule,
If Rothesay be deposed his high control?
His haughty spirit may not brook recal
Save at the hand of royalty. Say, brother,
Will you assume the high lieutenancy
Until my foolish son be brought to end
His levity and license? You are proved
In active government, are my right hand
In all affairs of state; help me in this,
And more than brother shall you be to me,
For much I need your aid in my affliction.
ALBANY.—I am unwilling to assume the power.
My nephew may become mine enemy,
Were I to dispossess him of his sway.
KING.—Yet who can fill the post so well as you?
You know the people, and their crying needs;
The nobles and their grievances; the clans,
Their feuds and their alliances. To you
Power is a plaything; you were born to rule,
And love the occupation. Happy thought,
That bids me to depute the power to you,
And save the honour of my hapless son.
ALBANY.—   Methinks to rule
Is but a thankless office at the best.
Press me no further; I'll have none of it.
KING.—You love me, brother?
ALBANY.—   Better than myself;
And "self," they say, is rooted to the core
In all mankind.
KING.—Then by your love for me
And mine, and by your loyalty, I beg
That you accept the lord-lieutenancy
Until my son be unto reason brought
And credit with the nation.
ALBANY.—   I consent.
'Tis with a heavy heart, for I had deemed
My active days were o'er; yet must I ask,

As a condition of my acquiescence,
That when my office is proclaimed you place
Within my hands a private warrant for
The apprehension of the Prince.   I ask
The writ for mine own safety ; shall employ
The powers entrusted me with lenity.

KING.—You would avoid a conflict with my son,
And would imprison him pending my pleasure?

ALBANY.—Ay ; and when captured, you shall be advised
With all due expedition, so that you
May visit him in his captivity,
Or order his removal to the Court,
As best may please your Majesty.

KING.—   'Tis well.
When we have caged this gay gallant of mine,
I'll bring him and his wife into our Court,
And with all honour shall entreat the twain
As Scotland's fairest, loftiest, and best.
It will go hard with me if I be foiled
In my attempt to join them heart to heart,
As they are joined already hand to hand ;
For daily converse strengthens Cupid's darts,
And I shall sequestrate them from the world
Until they learn to love.   'Tis a rare plan,
And suits my humour.   Come, my brother, come
Into our council chamber, to advise
This warrant of arrestment.   Albany !
Let him be treated with all gentleness
When he is taken.

ALBANY.—   With all gentleness
Shall he be treated, and yourself apprised
Where he shall be imprisoned.

KING.—   Albany !
You love the Prince, my son?

ALBANY.—   He is my nephew,
Your eldest son, the heir to Scotland's throne ;
Need I say more?

KING.—   Be very gentle with him
When he is captive.   He is but a youth ;
Haughty as youth will be, and proud, mayhap,
For high his lineage.   Like the eagle, he
May fret within his cage.   'Tis understood
You send me notice by swift messengers
When he is taken?

ALBANY.—   Brother, brother,—King !—
Whence comes this urgency?   Let me depart
Unto my private home ; you trust me not.

KING.—Nay, nay, forgive me ; I am sick at heart,
And there be times I know not what I say.
We do what we decide on for the best ;

And so 'tis best.   Who shall gainsay my words?
Yet he is very dear to me, my son,—
My winsome, haughty, thoughtless, fair-haired lad,—
To whom the world is sunshine, life and love,
Frolic and happiness.   Alas, alas !
Life has been only dreariness to me ; .
To me, a very cumberer of the ground,
Halting in mind and body, weak of soul,
Irresolute, and shrinking from the world.
No more on this.   Yet, as you love me, brother,
O love my boy ; but I do know you love him.
We 'll to the council chamber for this warrant.
Lend me your arm, good brother ; come, come, come.
                                        [*Exeunt.*

SCENE II.—*A room in the Castle of St Andrews.*   EARL DOUGLAS,
   his son ARCHIBALD DOUGLAS, *and* SIR WILLIAM LINDSAY.

LINDSAY.—Duke Albany?
E. DOUGLAS.—Has gone to Falkland.   Like a tiger he
      Crouches within his lair, and waits his victim.
LINDSAY.—Art sure, my Lord, that Rothesay is in Fife?
E. DOUGLAS.—Duke Albany has tracked him into Fife.
      Armed with the royal warrant, he is bold,
      Nor shuns responsibility ; besides
      He's now our lord-lieutenant, for the King
      Has cancelled Rothesay's office, and the Duke
      Grants warrant for his nephew's apprehension.
      'Twixt the King's warrant and the governor's
      The Prince's capture cannot be delayed,
      For he suspects not his disgrace and fall.
ARCHD. DOUGLAS.—O that my sister ne'er had seen his face !
LINDSAY.—And I, too, have a sister.
ARCHD. DOUGLAS.—Yes, he did win my sister by fair speech
      And sweet address ; did boldly gaze on her
      One moment, and the next would glance adown
      As though her very presence dazzled him.
      I marked their wooing ; I believed in him,
      As did my sister ; and I thought he loved her.
      Then came the marriage, then the honeymoon ;
      Next their return—alas ! a sad return
      For the young Princess.   On his words she hung
      Timid and fearful.   Narrowly I scanned
      Her countenance, and I could see she feared him.
      When he was merry, she would laugh with him
      In counterfeited glee ; 'twas pitiful
      To hear her voice.   When he turned fretful, she
      Hung o'er him tenderly, and every art
      Essayed to wean him from his savage mood.

Then she grew pale and thin, and restless too,
When he was absent. Evermore her thoughts
Seemed to be with her husband; but the light
Within her eyes was not the light of love,
But rather fear and sharp uneasiness.
I marked it all, indignant, for I pitied,
And pity still, my sister for her fate.

LINDSAY.—But in all this you only paint the life
Of wedded thousands.

ARCH. DOUGLAS.—Ay, but this victim is a Douglas, sir.
One day I entered, unannounced, their room.
My sister was in tears, and o'er her hung
Her husband; with his clenchéd fists he stood
Threat'ning and furious. I rushed between them.
Her cheek was reddened with a recent blow.
I swear it!—from her lips I wrung the truth
That the foul dastard dealt his gentle wife
A coward blow. Before the Prince I stood,
And cursed him in my father's name and mine,
And dared him to the combat. For an instant he
All undecided stood, but at the sight
Of his fair wife, dishevelled and in tears,
Wringing her hands, and moaning pitiful,
He sheathed his rapier, and the chamber left
With hurried step, and casting as he went
A baneful glance upon us both. O God!
But I could weep to think our noble house
Is to a villain such as this allied,
Though he be royal. O that I were set
Against him on some wild and lonesome moor,
None present save us twain; with blade in hand,
I'd so avenge my hapless sister's wrongs,
That through broad Scotland would the tidings ring
A wonder to all time.

Enter DUCHESS OF ROTHESAY *and* SIR JOHN RAMORNIE.

E. DOUGLAS.—Welcome, Ramornie;
Now by your hurried coming you have news
Of moment to disclose.

RAMORNIE.—My Lord, the Prince is captured, and by me.
Near to Strathtyrum was the goshawk trapped.

E. DOUGLAS.—I joy to hear it.

ARCH. DOUGLAS.—This is the happiest moment of my life.

LINDSAY.—Would I had been the captor; would that I
Were now his keeper.

DUCHESS OF ROTHESAY [*Aside*].—Alas!

E. DOUGLAS [*to Duchess*].—Now is the time, my daughter, for
revenge.
[*To Ramornie*]—Tell me the manner of his capture, sir.

RAMORNIE.—In Falkland dwells a certain light-o'-love,
    A former mistress of the Prince,—her name
    Is Catherine Graeme.   Within this woman's house
    Rothesay has dwelt since he forsook his wife,
    And there had he remained, no doubt, till now,
    Had not the coming of Duke Albany
    Caused his withdrawal.   Under cloud of night,
    Wellnigh a week agone, he left the town,
    And leisurely has through the district passed
    Engaged in falconry.   We tracked his course,
    Now here, now there, for slender was his escort
    And the way devious ; but 'twas evident
    This castle of Saint Andrews was his aim,
    For since the recent death of Bishop Trail
    He looks upon this castle as his own.
    An arméd force, by Albany's command,
    Was mine to intercept the Prince ; we met
    Near to Strathtyrum ; small resistance he
    And his weak escort offered, for amazed
    Were one and all when the King's warrant I
    Produced for his arrestment.   Little more
    Have I to add ; he's in this castle now,
    My prisoner ; say, shall we hold him here,
    Or send him on to Falkland to the Duke?
DUCHESS.—Here let him bide, for hither have I come
    At his command.   This castle is his own ;
    And, till the pleasure of the King be known,
    Shall I be guaranty for his safe-keeping.
LINDSAY.—Bring him before us ; I'd have speech of him,
    Ere we decide on his disposal.
ARCH. DOUGLAS.—   I
    Shall meet him face to face—it is my right—
    Within these walls ; and, sword in hand, shall carve
    My soul's revenge upon him !
E. DOUGLAS.—   Silence, boy ;
    You are a brawler.   This shall I advise,—
    Nay, more, command,—for in this matter we
    Are secondary actors.   Who is set
    The Governor of Scotland in the room
    Of Scotland's Prince?   'Tis now Duke Albany,
    To whom the royal warrant was entrusted ;
    And thus into the hands of Albany
    Shall Rothesay be confided.   Nay, no more,
    My daughter, I have said ; no more, my son,
    I answer for you both, and for myself.
    The Prince shall on to Falkland, to the care
    Of his devoted uncle Albany.
RAMORNIE.—You carry reason in your speech, my lord,
    I'll on to Falkland with my prisoner.
LINDSAY.—In better hands the Prince cannot be placed.

ARCH. DOUGLAS.—In truth, good father, you have said aright
    Let us confide our Jovite to his uncle.
DUCHESS.—O hear me father, brother, and good sirs,
    Send not my husband to Duke Albany,
    That stony-hearted and ambitious man,
    Remorseless, cruel, and unprincipled.
    What ! know you not the very fiends in hell
    Are angels in comparison with him ?
    For fiends do band together, but this man
    Stands solitary on a pinnacle
    Of treachery and the mad lust for power,
    And in no man confides what he contrives
    Against his enemies.   O trust him not ;
    Remember he is brother to the King,
    But not the King.   O keep my husband here,
    And notify his capture to the King,
    Then your responsibility shall cease
    Whate'er betide.   His Majesty is meek,
    Honest, and merciful ; into his hands
    Gladly shall I confide my erring lord,
    But not to Albany's.
E. DOUGLAS.—   Daughter, no more,
    Thou art degenerate ; until this day
    A Douglas never did a wrong forgive,
    Or kiss the hand that struck a coward blow.
    If thou hast pardoned Rothesay, I have not,
    And in the Lord-Lieutenant's hands he shall
    Be set at pleasure of his Majesty.
    Come, sirs, let us provide a proper guard
    For this illustrious son-in-law of mine,
    And on to Falkland with him ere the night
    Darkens the lengthy road, for the day wears.
                 [*Exeunt all but the* DUCHESS OF ROTHESAY.
DUCHESS.—O, heart of woman, changeable and weak !
    Since I became a wedded wife have I
    A thousand times declared that I do hate him.
    Have I not cause?   He has neglected me,
    Treated my taunts with cold indifference ;
    And to my prayers for but a little love,
    A little courtesy, a kindly glance,
    He answered with a sneer,—my day is past !
    The fire that once within his bosom glowed
    For me is quenched ; alas that it is so.
    I cannot hate him ; in this one respect
    I prove apostate from the Douglas faith.
    I am no Douglas, but a Stuart now,
    Therefore I pardon him who is my husband.
    O, Rothesay, freely do I pardon thee.
    Ah ! would to God that I could die for thee,
    If thou art doomed to death.   I'll to the Duke

His uncle, and in Falkland rest awhile
To see the issue of this daring stroke.
Come, resolution, to my laggard wit,
And teach me to encounter Albany
With craft 'gainst craft; 'tis for my husband's self
That I do battle. O ! may heaven approve
The issue, and restore my husband's love
Into its rightful channel. If his wife
Save through device his coveted young life,
Then gratitude may ardent love renew,
When in his adverse fate he proves me true.   [*Exit.*

SCENE III.—*Falkland Castle.* ROTHESAY *in Prison.*

ROTHESAY.—Another miserable night agone !
How cold it is, how drear ! These stony bounds
Mock my estate ; the heir to Scotland's throne
Entrapped, degraded thus ! Yet I have slept
Upon this cruel couch, till the foul drip
From overhead awaked me. Woe is me,
What have I done to be entreated thus ?
See ! through the loophole of this gloomy cell
The first faint gleam of day ; and I do hear,
Enraptured at the birth of the young day,
The music of the merle, and nearer still
The note of red-breast more deliberate,
Yet passing sweet. Alas ! but ye are free,
While I— A dreary chill creeps through my veins,
And I do hunger. Oftentimes it chanced,
When in the chase or falconry engaged,
That I have hungered, and for very joy
Have laughed to find it so ; never till now
Did hunger in its dread reality
Lay hold upon me. Like a rav'ning monster
It gnaws my vitals, will not be appeased,
And goads me nigh to madness. Can it be
They have forgot me ?
                              Ho ! ye knaves without !
I would have speech of you. This awful silence !
This is a living grave ! Ho, jailers, ho !
              [*Beats loudly on the door, and enter the
                    Jailers* SELKIRK *and* WRIGHT.

SELKIRK.—What would you, master?
WRIGHT.—Cease this clamour, sir,
Else we shall set the gyves upon your limbs,
And gag you into silence.
ROTHESAY.—How now, knaves !
A murrain on ye both ; go, bring me food,
For I do hunger ; bring me wine, and fetch

My cloak, for in this narrow slimy cell
Have I been thrust without the decencies
Or means of keeping life within me ;—go,
And quickly, ere resentment urges me
To dub you traitors to my royal line.

SELKIRK.—We serve Duke Albany, and he is royal.

ROTHESAY.—The Duke knows not that I am prisoned here;
Or, if he knew, he durst not have me starve.
How mean you?

WRIGHT.—Sir, our meaning is, in brief,
To act as it was ordered by the Duke ;
Here you remain our prisoner, without
Food, drink, or clothing, till his pleasure be
To grant you freedom.

ROTHESAY.—That may never come.

SELKIRK.—Ay, surely it will come; ay, it must come
In one way or another.

ROTHESAY.—   Death will grant
Me freedom—death by hunger, thirst, and cold.
Is this your meaning?

WRIGHT.—   An' it please you, sir,
What need to bandy words ?   Let us withdraw.

ROTHESAY.—Stay, jailers, stay.   O this is terrible !
Stay, 'tis the Prince of Scotland pleads.   O men,
Have ye not sons? think of your flesh and blood
Imprisoned on these terms,—thrust in a cell,
Dark, slimy, stone-engirdled, horrible,—
With ne'er a morsel of sustaining food,
Without a cup of water to allay
Thirst's quick-devouring fever.   Ye would pity
Your sons in such a strait, then pity me.

WRIGHT.—Pity is duty's adversary ; we
Are faithful to our trust.

ROTHESAY.—   Ye both are Scots—
The king of Scotland is my father !—all
Swear fealty to the crown, to Scotland's king,—
And I, his heir-apparent, next himself,
Do stand most precious in our subjects' sight.
Thus are ye bound in faith and trust to me,
And I command that you obey me now.

WRIGHT.—'Tis needless—say no more.

ROTHESAY.—   Short-sighted men !
Ye blink like owls in the broad light of day.
What ! see you not it is impossible
That Albany can dare to murder me?
If so it were, the nation to a man
Would rise, and take such terrible revenge
On him and you, that never to all time
Would history forget it.   Let me go ;
When I am free you shall have gold and rank,

Such as befit your service ; let me go,
And I shall pay you with sweet gratitude,
Backed by a monarch's thanks.
SELKIRK.—Idly you rave ;
Our master is Duke Albany, and he
Is king and master both.
ROTHESAY.— When I am free,
Revenge shall be my study. Never more
Shall Albany be Scotland's governor.
But I wear faint. O for a little food !
Good sirs, go quickly, bring a little food.
For every ounce of food you bring to me,
I'll pay you back an hundred overweight
In gold, and in the grateful balance cast
My thanks besides,—the thanks of Scotland's Prince.
WRIGHT.—Enough, time wears, and we must go.
ROTHESAY (*seizing his robe*).—
One moment ; but one moment ! Sure, the birds
Lack not their food ; the vilest beasts that creep
This teeming earth of ours, have all their share ;
Then, wherefore keep from me what nature gives,
Until their latest breath, to one and all ?
If 'tis my life you seek, I stand before you ;
Despatch me if you will, I am content ;
But doom me not to die of rav'ning want,
And to become, ere kindly death arrives,
A thing abhorrent to the eyes of nature.
Ah ! you are pitiless ; well were you chosen
For such a task as this.
WRIGHT.— Release your grasp,
Else will I dash you to the ground.
ROTHESAY.— Your dagger—
Lend me your dagger ; if you fear to rob
Me of my life, myself shall do the deed.
WRIGHT.—Take this—and this—you feeble whining fool.
                    [*Beats him ; they struggle, and* ROTHESAY *is
                            thrown heavily to the ground.*
SELKIRK.—I fear that you have killed him.
WRIGHT.— Nay, he breathes.
Shall I despatch him ? I've a mind to do it,
And end our watch.
            Enter ALBANY, *by a secret door.*
ALBANY.—Hold, knave ! What, have you killed him ?
Have I not ordered that no hack nor mark
Shall on his body show ? Have you forgot,
Or are you wearied of your life ?
WRIGHT.— He lives ;
He is but stunned. See, your grace, he revives.
ALBANY.—Withdraw ; but keep ye both within due call.
                    [*Exeunt* SELKIRK *and* WRIGHT.

I have thee at my feet, mine enemy !
Revenge, thou dainty morsel, thou art mine ;
Not to consume with ill-considered haste,
But leisurely ; that so I may extract
Truest enjoyment from its rarity !
Is this mine enemy? this slender lad,
This willow wand ?   Is this, forsooth, a power?
Now let me trace his features, while he lies
Passive and motionless.   He has self-will,
That well I know, and obstinacy too,
And pride of birth ; but strength of purpose, none.
He is a man of pleasure at the best ;
And had he chosen to subject his will
To mine, he might have reigned this country's king ;
But from the day he dared to pit himself
In arrogance 'gainst me, his doom was read.
But, soft—he rouses.   David, Duke of Rothesay,
Arise ; 'tis Albany who speaks to thee.

ROTHESAY.—   [*Slowly rising.*
They struck me to the ground !   They dared to strike
The son of him, the anointed of the Lord.
I do remember all.   Duke Albany,
Explain thy presence here.   I do not bid
Thee welcome, for it is to thee I owe
This chamber and this treatment.

ALBANY.—Nephew, nay—

ROTHESAY.—I do not term thee *uncle*, Albany ;
For 'tis a word that kinsmanship engrafts
On courtesy ; and that is dead for us.
Nephew is sad misnomer from thy lips.

ALBANY.—Then, Duke of Rothesay, Scotland's noblest Prince,
I come to visit thee in thy retirement,
And humbly to inquire if thou art lodged
In manner suitable.   Hast aught complaint?

ROTHESAY.—None, Duke of Albany.

ALBANY.—A royal residence !   These massive walls
Encircle Scotland's heir, and hold him safe
Against his enemies.   So far 'tis well.

ROTHESAY.—So far 'tis well.

ALBANY.—And yet the air is chill and deadly.   Thou
Art thinly clad ; hast aught petition for
Soft couch or warmer clothing ?

ROTHESAY.—None from thee.

ALBANY.—I trust the keepers bring abundant food,
And of fair quality, for my Lord Duke ?

ROTHESAY.—I ask thee for none other than they bring.

ALBANY.—And water?

ROTHESAY [*pointing to the roof*].—Do I lack water here?

ALBANY.—Hast aught petition?

ROTHESAY.—One alone, Lord Duke.

This princely cell thou hast assigned to me
Ought to be mine. 'Tis now my all on earth.
Leave me to solitude ; I ask no more.
ALBANY.—Rude lad ! and thou wouldst parley thus with me ?
I hold thee in the hollow of my hand ;
And coarser natures at a single blow
Might glut them in a barbarous revenge,
But I refine upon thy punishment,
And do consign thee to a living death.
Here thou shalt pine and starve, and slowly die.
Here thou shalt rot until thou pray'st for death,—
A glad release from that foul thing, thyself.
Boy, I do hate thee ! Thou hast hated me
Since first the dawn of manhood 'gan to clothe
Thy saucy face. I know it. I have marked
Thine eye, thy knitted brows, thy countenance ;
And hate breeds hate. Far better for thyself
Had'st thou been confident that Albany
Was thy true friend ; far better for thyself
To have absorbed thee in thy junkettings,
Debaucheries, and riots, and have left
The government to me,—to the manner born
To rule. But, no ! Thou wouldst be Governor,
Supplanting me,—Ay, me ; thou malapert,—
With taunt and sneer, and open mockery.
Boy, I do tell thee ne'er a taunt or sneer,
And ne'er a silly trick of mockery,
But I have hoarded in my injured breast ;
And now the hour of my revenge is come.
Go, lay thee on thy stony couch and starve !
And now, farewell, and think on Albany.
                    [*Departs by the secret door.*
ROTHESAY.—Albany ?
          [*Rushes to the door and beats it with his hands,*
              then falls to the ground.

———

SCENE IV.—*A Wood near Falkland Castle. Enter* CATHERINE
GRAEME.

CATHERINE.—And yonder frowning pile possesses him !
Poor youth ! 'Tis said he sickens nigh to death,
And raves in his delirium. O that I
Stood by his fevered couch to tend and soothe him ;
To listen to his accents, though they be
Of reason robbed ; to gaze upon his face,
To touch his hand, to minister to him,
To lend those thousand aids that baffle death,
And beckon back again departed health.

This, this were heaven to me, for I do love him,
Though mine be love unlawful.   Can I live
Forgetful of his tenderness, his vows,
His protestations that in me alone
His happiness was centred ; that the claims
Of birth alone forbad the marriage tie ?
I did believe him, I believe him still ;
And if for him I lost my fair repute,
In my great fall the greater was my love.
May God forgive us both, but chiefly me,
For chiefly have I erred.

Enter DUCHESS OF ROTHESAY.

DUCHESS.—Madam, thy name ?
CATHERINE.—I know not, madam, who requires my name.
DUCHESS.—A woman most unfortunate am I,
    The Duke of Rothesay's wife.
CATHERINE.—And I am Catherine Graeme ; thou know'st me not.
    I would away, my household duties call
    Me to my home.
DUCHESS.—Stay, Catherine Graeme, with thee would I have speech.
    'Tis thee I seek,—would thy assistance crave,—
    To aid my prisoned husband.
CATHERINE.—Prisoned, and fever-stricken, so 'tis told.
DUCHESS.—Prisoned, but languishing for lack of food ;
    If it be that starvation is disease,
    Then is he fevered well nigh to his death.
CATHERINE.—Can this be true ?   O I am strangely stirred.
DUCHESS.—On from Saint Andrews have I hurried here
    To crave his prisoner of Albany,
    And I made offer to accompany
    The Prince to good King Robert's residence,
    But I am baffled ; honied words have I
    Receivéd of the Duke, and wreathéd smiles,
    And studied courtesy, but nothing more.
    The man is most malignant in his hate,
    And serpent-like in murd'rous wisdom he.
    I craved an interview with mine own husband,
    But 'twas denied me ; nay, it was deferred,
    To this intent that I am kept from him,
    And of set purpose.
CATHERINE.—Can this purpose be —— ?
DUCHESS.—Listen !   I am the self-invited guest
    Of Albany in yonder gloomy pile,
    And one there dwells within the castle walls
    Friendly to me and mine, from whom I learn
    The sum of this sad history.   The Prince
    Is doomed, the pride and glory of his youth
    Is coveted, but 'tis a bloodless death
    They destine for him ; and behind the plea

Of fell disease they shield the murd'rous deed.
Thou know'st the eastern tower that gloomily
Frowns o'er the castle? there is Rothesay prisoned.
They hold him in a dungeon dank and drear,
Without the necessaries of dear life ;
Water and food are both denied ; his prayers
Are all unheeded, or, if listened to,
Are gloated over by malignant ears.
O God, that this is so,—that I am here !
Here, wellnigh by my husband's side, and yet
Powerless to aid him !
       Yesterday I walked
Warily by the tower where he is caged.
Close to its base there is a loophole set,
That draws the niggard light to the foul cell
Which keeps my husband. I approached the loop,
And lift the ivy screen aside. I gazed
Within ; at first mine eyes beheld him not,
But soon, accustomed to the gloom, I saw—
In pity saw—him seated on his couch,
His face upon his hands. I spoke to him ;
'Twas in a whisper, lest his guards might hear.
Then, on the sudden, at my voice he raised
His face ; his eyes met mine. O Jesu, dear,
That I should see my husband's features thus !
I may not dwell upon the scene. Enough,
That they do starve him, that he must have food,
And on the instant, or his life is lost.

CATHERINE.—You carried food to him ?

DUCHESS.—   Alas, alas,
But I am helpless here ; my steps are watched ;
A guard is set upon me. I contrived
Again to near the loop, with food concealed
Under my mantle. Lo ! when I approached
A warder hung upon my every step,
And I was baffled. Help me ; be my friend
In mine extremity.

CATHERINE.—   Lady, you demand
What is impossible.

DUCHESS.—   Nay ; I am told
That you have access to the castle when
You choose to pass the gates.

CATHERINE.—   True ; I am poor—
My duties lead me often to the castle.

DUCHESS.—You know the gloomy tower where Rothesay lies
Prisoned and starving ?

CATHERINE.—   I do know the tower,
And in a mood inquisitive have gazed
In happier days down through the narrow loop
Into the cell.

DUCHESS.— Then, O be merciful,
And through that loop send Rothesay precious life.

CATHERINE.—You would that I convey supplies to him
By virtue of mine insignificance?

DUCHESS.—Ah! choose not bitter words; give help to him,
And I will bless thee to my dying day.

CATHERINE.—Lady, implore me not.

DUCHESS.— Upon my knees
I do implore thee for thy priceless aid.

CATHERINE.—Lady, arise; you shall not, cannot kneel
To such as me. How! are you not aware
I was his leman once upon a time?

DUCHESS.—I knew it, Catherine, ere I came to thee.

CATHERINE.—And—what is even harder still for you,
His wedded wife, to know—he loves me still.

DUCHESS.—I know it. Sad has been my wedded life;
In mine extremity I do confess it.
My husband has despised me, lightlied me,
And, worse than all, he has deserted me,
Proving unfaithful to his marriage vows.
Yet I do love him! am I not his wife?
Can I say more than this?—*I still do love him!*
And here upon my bended knees I pray
To thee, my rival, to have pity on him,
And save his precious life.

CATHERINE (*raising her up*).—Rise, lady; you have conquered, for
your love
Is greater than mine own. I pity him,
And shall attempt to aid him in his need;
I pity him, and sorrow for your woes.
O may your sorrow soon be changed to joy,
And happier days remain in store for you.
Come, lady, come, and let us twain contrive
How best to baffle Nature's enemies;
For this attempt my head may forfeit be—
Whate'er the penalty—I am resolved. [*Exeunt.*

SCENE V.—*Falkland Castle. Before Rothesay's Tower*
SELKIRK *and* WRIGHT.

SELKIRK.—'Tis strange, but he is as tenacious of his life as a cat.
He may not have nine lives, but there's more than one life in him.

WRIGHT.—Had he ninety, I would soon end them all, were it
but left to me.

SELKIRK.—The Duke suspects that he receives secret supplies,
hence our instructions to watch the dungeon loop. This must be
so, else how could our prisoner exist so long? Can a man live on

air, or on light, or on sand, or on a filthy water drop? There's mystery here, I trow, and it rests with us to clear it up.

WRIGHT.—Yet he was well nourished in flesh when first he fell into our hands; but now, i'faith, he has become so thin, that I fear he may soon escape us by creeping out of this aperture. Ah, these aristocrats, how I do hate them! How I gloried to hear our prisoner on his coming here first demand, then implore, then entreat, then pray, then howl in frenzy, for food, for water, for pity. Pity! that's a scarce commodity among gentlemen of our profession. And now he has become quiet—he heeds us not, he petitions us not; depend on't he has secret supplies, and it will prove to our credit if we can detect the source.

SELKIRK.—A curse on the man, woman, or child who dares to interfere here, and tamper with the course of justice. Duke Albany would give short shrift to the culprit.

WRIGHT.—Soft! some one comes. 'Tis a woman; let us pass aside and keep concealed. Let us take ourselves round the tower, and bide within hearing distance; the moth draws nigh to the candle.

[*Exeunt.*

Enter CATHERINE GRAEME, *enveloped in a large mantle.*

CATHERINE.—Night, open-armed, descends upon the earth.
    The rooks are wending homeward, and the bat
    Wheels in the twilight on capricious wing.
    Nature is waiting slumber—all is still—
    I'll venture to the loop. 'Tis now the hour
    When vigilance is lulled, and in the halls
    The warders love to loiter and carouse.
    Ah's me! this awful stillness. I can hear
    The throbbing of my heart!—Stay! did I hear
    A footstep? Nay, 'twas but the distant tramp
    Of sentinel upon his watch. A whisper?
    'Twas but the distant ripple of the brook
    That glides beyond the castle. O my heart
    Be still, and turn not traitor to myself.
    Be brave in this extremity of need,
    Else will my task miscarry. Did I hear
    A voice? 'Twas but the beetle's drowsy hum
    Mysterious in the air. Am I turned coward?
    The moaning of the wind upon the hills
    May next disturb me. Let me close mine ears
    'Gainst all that mounts the silence of the air,
    And rides atilt my fears. I'll to my duty.

[*Kneels down and gazes through the aperture
of the Dungeon.*

I cannot see him! Ah! this horrid darkness
That broods funereal-like upon his cell!
Perhaps he sleeps the awful sleep of death.
Dost slumber, Duke of Rothesay? Oh awake!

Stay, I can hear
The ceaseless drip of water on the floor,
Measured and slow, Time's regulator there ;
And I can hear—yes—I do hear his voice !
So faint and weak, I recognised it not
For Rothesay's !   Yes—he speaks to me—he speaks !
So feeble and unearthly is his voice,
That pain and terror strike me to the heart
Ev'n as I listen.   David, thou art weak,
And faint, and cold—I know it all—oh, drag
Thy limbs across the floor, and come to me,
And I shall give thee food.   See, here is milk,
And with this slender reed shalt thou contrive—

> [SELKIRK *and* WRIGHT *glide forward, and*
> SELKIRK *places his hand upon her shoulder*
> *—she turns her head.*

Alas ! my hope has perished—lost, lost, lost !

———

SCENE VI.—*Falkland Castle.   Ante-room of the Chapel.   The back-ground of the chamber is heavily draped.*   DUKE ALBANY *and the* DUCHESS OF ROTHESAY.

ALBANY.—I cannot probe to the bottom of your charge.
DUCHESS.—Release my husband, and my heavy charge
 Shall I discharge anon.   Duke Albany,
 You have no warrant for this thing you do.
ALBANY.—I hold the warrant of our gracious King.
DUCHESS.—To apprehend, but never to maltreat.
ALBANY.—How, madam, you are bold !   What ! know you not
 The King confides his son to me.   The realm
 Cries shame upon your husband ;—so did you ;—
 So do the nobles.   To my vigilance
 Is Scotland's heir entrusted.   Have a care !
 I am Lieutenant in Duke Rothesay's room.
DUCHESS.—The King is generous and kind ; he waits
 The coming of his son.   Your task it was
 To apprehend my husband, and convey
 Him to his father's custody ; but never
 Were you his constituted keeper.   Sir,
 Beware ! you know not I know all !   Beware
 A woman's wrath !   That you have overstepped
 Your high commission when you caged my lord
 You know ; but in the reckless depths you plunged
 When you consigned him to a monstrous death,
 And left him in your dungeon cells to starve.
ALBANY.—'Tis a foul charge, and I deny it, lady.

I am no murderer.　Malignant sickness
Seized hold upon the Prince.　Am I to blame
For Nature's chastisement?
DUCHESS.—Name Nature not to me.　I do believe
There's ne'er a spark of human kindness glows
Within your bosom.　Oh! black-hearted man,
False is your nature! bitterness and gall
Are your best composites!　I fear you not,
But I distrust you utterly.　My sp'rit
Recoils from you as from some deadly thing;
That you are venomous I know.　Release
My husband, and I shall unsay my words.
ALBANY.—Proceed, and welcome, madam.
DUCHESS.—　　　　　　　　　　　　I demand,
In good King Robert's name, and in mine own,
And in the name of Scotland's royal heir,
And in the nation's name, that you release
Duke Rothesay.
ALBANY.—　　　　　　Wherefore, madam, may I ask?
He is well housed and well protected here.
DUCHESS.—Your hardihood unsexes me.　Desist!
Else will I curse you in your flesh and blood,
Your family and store, till evil fortune,
Like to a bloodhound, hunts you to the doom,
And forces you to wail at God's decrees.
What! know I not you are ambition's slave?
That Rothesay stands in your ambition's way?
What! know I not you starve him to the death,
Yet would give out he dies by Nature's law?
Oh, Albany! before it be too late,
Release my husband, give him to mine arms,
And I will bless you while I live.　Remember,
The King his father, and myself, his wife,
Have influence with him.　Gladly will we
Advise him to renounce th' uneasy craft
Of government to you, and in the field
Display his prowess and receive his spurs;
So shall your interests undivided be,
And each shall on the other proudly lean.
ALBANY.—I hear you to the end most patiently;
But since Duke Rothesay passed within these walls
His treatment has been all he best deserves.
You ask for his release?—*he is released.*
You stand amazed!　Restrain your passion, madam,
'Tis true; the Prince has left his prison bounds,
Shall enter them no more.
DUCHESS.—May God bestow his blessing upon you!
O royal Albany!　When shall I see
My husband? let me clasp him in mine arms.
O happiness to know that he is free!

ALBANY.—Shall I delay the joyous meeting?   Nay—
 Ho there, within! draw back this drapery,
 The Duchess Rothesay enters.
>   [*The curtains are drawn back, displaying the
>   Chapel Royal draped in black.   In the centre
>   a bier, whereon the dead body of* DUKE
>   ROTHESAY *is laid.   Attendants with candles
>   line the walls, and round the bier stand friars
>   also with candles.   They begin to chaunt in a
>   deep tone.*

ALBANY.—Your husband waits your coming, noble lady.
DUCHESS (*rushing forward, and gazing on the face of the dead*).—
 My husband!

www.ingramcontent.com/pod-product-compliance
Lightning Source LLC
Chambersburg PA
CBHW030900260626
47169CB00008B/2621